Felix the
Fluffy Kitten
and Other Kitten Tales

Contents

Felix
the Fluffy Kitten

Special thanks to Mary Hooper
To Daisy – another fluffy kitten

Chapter One

Jodie Taylor woke with a start and remembered what day it was. She jumped out of bed and ran straight downstairs in her pyjamas.

"Happy birthday, sleepy head!" her mum said as Jodie bounced into the kitchen. "I was just about to come and wake you up. Fancy sleeping in late today!"

"I was awake at five o'clock, wondering what presents I'd get," Jodie said, rubbing her eyes. "But then I snoozed off again."

Jodie's dad came into the kitchen with his coat on. "Happy birthday, love!" He looked at his watch. "I'll just about have time to watch you open your presents."

Jodie looked excitedly at the pile of cards and presents beside her cereal bowl. She sat down and began opening them.

There was a soft pink sweater from her nana, a computer game from Uncle Jack and a rucksack in the shape of a lamb from Auntie Joyce. But nothing from her mum and dad.

Jodie looked at them, surprised. Then her dad winked at her mum. What was going on?

"Now open the cards!" he said.

Jodie tore open her cards. There were eight of them – the same number as her new age.

At the bottom of the pile was an ordinary-looking brown envelope with Jodie's name on it. "This doesn't look like a card," she said.

Mr Taylor peered at it. "It doesn't look like anything much."

"Looks like a bill," said Mrs Taylor, trying not to smile.

Jodie opened the envelope and pulled

out a small white square of paper. On it
was written:

IOU one kitten.

Jodie looked at her mum and dad in
astonishment. "What does this mean?"

"It means," said Mrs Taylor, smiling,

"that your dad and I owe you one birthday kitten – and we're going to collect it later."

Jodie gave a squeal of delight. "Really?" This was what she'd dreamed of for ages. But her mum and dad had always said no. Until now!

Mr Taylor did up his coat. "Mum's taking you to see a lady called Mrs Dent after school," he said. "She has a litter of kittens ready to go to new homes." He dropped a kiss on Jodie's head. "Got to rush. Have a lovely day!" And he left to go to work.

"A kitten," Jodie breathed. "A real live kitten." She gave her mum a hug.

Mrs Taylor smiled, then she said, "Dad and I think you're old enough now to look after a pet of your own, Jodie."

"Oh, I am, I am!" Jodie said.

"So it's up to you to look after the kitten," Mrs Taylor went on. "You know how busy Dad and I are at the moment. We don't have time to feed and groom a pet or . . ." she pulled a face ". . . clear up any messes."

"Oh, there won't be any messes," Jodie said. She knew lots about pets and loved reading stories about cats. "Kittens are really clean. They're house-trained by their mothers from the moment they're born."

"I'm glad to hear it," said Mrs Taylor as she swished around the sink and gave it a little extra polish. "Because you know I can't bear any mess."

Jodie, used to her mum's neat and tidy ways, hardly heard her. She was getting a kitten! She was getting a kitten of her very own. She could hardly wait!

Chapter Two

"Oh, they're all lovely!" Jodie said, as five tiny kittens played about her feet. There were three fluffy grey kittens, like their mum, and two sweet black and white ones with pink noses.

Jodie sighed deeply. "I'm *never* going to be able to choose!" She got down on the floor and picked up each kitten in turn. "Oh, I don't know!" she wailed.

Jodie's mum smiled. "Can you help, Mrs Dent?"

"They're all good, clean little kittens," Mrs Dent said. "But the short-haired black and whites would be easier to care for. The grey kittens, being long-haired, will need lots more grooming."

"Oh, I won't mind doing that," Jodie said. "I shall love combing *my* kitten." She held up one of the grey fluffies. "This one has the bluest eyes. And he's *really* fluffy!"

The kitten looked at Jodie and miaowed. *Choose me!*

Jodie laughed and put him down so she could look at the other kittens again. But she kept coming back to the fluffiest one.

The kitten went up to Jodie and rubbed his face against her ankle. "You look nice," he purred. "I'd miss my mum and my brothers and sisters – but I wouldn't mind coming home with you."

"I really think you'll have to make up your mind, love," Jodie's mum said. "I'm sure Mrs Dent has other things to do."

Jodie watched as the kittens tumbled about, each trying to look the sweetest.

"Come on, Jodie," said Mrs Taylor.

The fluffiest kitten climbed onto Jodie's trainer, mewing up at her. And . . . well, if a kitten could smile, he was doing it.

Jodie's heart melted. "OK, I want . . ." She took a deep breath then scooped up the fluffiest kitten. "This one! I love him to bits already."

Delighted, the kitten pushed his head into Jodie's neck. "Good choice," he purred.

"At last!" said Mrs Taylor.

"What are you going to call him, dear?" Mrs Dent asked, smiling.

Jodie thought hard. "I'm going to call him Felix," she said. She gave Felix a cuddle. "You're my fluffy Felix."

Tired from all his kitten capers, Felix closed his eyes, burrowed his nose into the crook of Jodie's arm and went to sleep.

Jodie's mum paid Mrs Dent, and Felix

was put in the pet carrying box they'd bought from the local pet shop on the way.

Jodie looked down at her sleeping kitten and smiled. "Look," she said. "He's so fluffy that you can hardly tell which way round he is!"

"He does have a wonderful thick coat," Mrs Dent agreed. "The thickest I've ever seen. You'll need a special comb for grooming him. And he'll need combing every day." She wrote down the details for Jodie.

Jodie thanked her and gave Felix a gentle stroke before closing the carrying box.

Still sleeping, Felix purred. What a lovely life he was going to have with his new family . . .

On the way home, Jodie and her mum popped into Pearce's Perfect Pets in the high street.

"Oh, you've brought your new kitten in to see me," said Mr Pearce, the owner.

Felix allowed himself to be lifted out of his basket, put on the counter and shown off to Mr Pearce.

"Well!" said Mr Pearce. "What a fine kitten – and such a wonderful coat."

Felix preened himself, purring loudly. He could get used to all this praise!

Jodie nodded, pleased. "He's lovely, isn't he?"

"You don't want to sell him, do you?" Mr Pearce joked.

"No way!" Jodie said. "We've come in to buy a special comb for grooming long-haired cats." She gave Mr Pearce

17

the piece of paper Mrs Dent had given her, with the type of comb written on it.

"I don't think I've got one in stock," said Mr Pearce. "But I'll order one for you. Jot down your phone number and I'll ring you when it's in."

"I hope it won't take long," Jodie's mum said, writing down their number. "I want that grey fluff combed out before it gets shed all over the house!"

Mr Pearce tickled Felix behind his ears. "With a thick coat like that, I reckon you'd soon comb enough fluff off him to knit yourself a woolly jumper!" he joked.

Jodie laughed. "I just want to keep him looking good."

"I tell you what," Mr Pearce said. "He's such a handsome kitten that I'd like to take his photograph to put in my window. I'm sure it would attract a lot of attention. I'll give you the comb

19

and a smart new collar in return. How's that?"

"Great!" said Jodie. "Can we, Mum?"

Mrs Taylor nodded. "I can't see why not," she said.

Felix began to wash around his face so that he'd look his best for the photograph.

"Why don't you choose a collar while I go and get my camera?" said Mr Pearce.

Jodie held a red and a green collar next to Felix, then chose the red one. She was carefully putting it on him when Mr Pearce came back with his camera.

Felix just loved attention. Everyone in

20

the shop was watching him now. "How about this?" he purred, looking over his shoulder, his tail up straight. "Or this?" he miaowed, rolling on his back and looking up at the camera, his blue eyes wide. "Have you ever seen anything so sweet?"

"I think he knows he's being snapped," Mr Pearce said, grinning. "He's posing like a model. He thinks he's one of those supermodels."

Supermodel? Superkitten, more like, Felix thought.

Chapter Three

"You'll have to try to keep Felix off this sofa, Jodie," Mrs Taylor said a couple of days later.

Jodie had just come in from school and was sitting watching TV, with Felix on her lap.

Mrs Taylor dabbed at the sofa with a damp cloth, then frowned at the grey fluff she'd gathered up. "Dad sat down wearing his new suit and got it covered in grey hairs this morning," she went on.

"Sorry," Jodie said. "I'll try and brush some of the loose fluff out of Felix's coat later." She was going to make do with an old blue hairbrush until the special comb arrived at the pet shop.

Tutting a little under her breath, Mrs Taylor went over to the vacuum cleaner in the corner. "And this old vacuum cleaner of ours is hopeless!" she added.

"Shall I have a go with it?" Jodie offered, feeling guilty at the extra work Felix's fluff was making for her mum.

23

Mrs Taylor shook her head. "It's much too heavy for you to lug around, love. It's too heavy for me, come to that!" She plugged in the big old machine and switched it on.

Felix, who'd been snoozing, sat bolt upright. *What* was that horrible roaring noise? He jumped down and made a dash for the stairs. Pale grey fluff hung in the air as he ran . . .

It was Saturday and Jodie was taking her time in the bathroom. She didn't have to rush to school this morning and could play with her new kitten all day.

Felix had decided to keep Jodie

company while she showered, and was perched on the edge of the bath. He bobbed from side to side, dabbing his paw in the drops of water. "Why can't I catch these little round silvery things?" he miaowed sharply. It was very annoying!

Jodie turned off the shower and put a dollop of soapy foam on the edge of the bath for Felix to play with.

Felix looked at the white froth. He reached out a paw – but the bit he touched seemed to disappear. Very odd.

He leaned over to sniff the strange stuff – and jumped back in surprise, sneezing as tiny soapy bubbles flew up

his nose. Felix lost his balance and slid into the bath, a wisp of foam still on his nose.

"Oh, Felix!" Jodie cried. "You silly puss!"

Jodie couldn't stop laughing as she lifted Felix out of the bath.

Then she noticed the hairs that had

flown off Felix as he'd skidded into the bath. She grabbed a cloth and quickly wiped them up before her mum noticed. Jodie could hear the vacuum cleaner on again, downstairs.

Felix had been with the Taylors for just over a week now, and he had settled in really well. But there was one big problem: his fluff!

Felix's lovely thick coat shed oodles of fluffy hair wherever Felix went. And Mrs Taylor was *not* pleased about it.

Jodie got dressed and took Felix into her bedroom. "Time to brush out some of that fluff," she said to him, setting him down on her bed.

She went to find the old blue hairbrush. But when she came back, Felix had vanished. Then she noticed a fluffy tail, fat as a squirrel's, sticking out of the duvet. "I can see you!" she called.

Jodie flung back the duvet to find Felix crouched down ready to pounce. He leapt into the air, scrabbled up her back and landed on her shoulder. "You're back! Let's play!" he miaowed loudly.

As Jodie collapsed onto the bed, giggling, her mum appeared in the doorway.

"Just look at all that fluff on your bedclothes, Jodie," Mrs Taylor said

frowning. "You'd better change them. And don't you think it's about time you started grooming that kitten? If you combed out all that loose fluff it wouldn't come out all over the house!"

"I'm going to, Mum – right now," Jodie said, and held up the brush to show her.

With a sigh, Mrs Taylor went back to her cleaning. Pulling Felix onto her lap, Jodie gently began to stroke the brush along his back.

But as far as Felix was concerned, the bristly blue creature was trying to attack him! He sprang round. "How dare you!" he hissed, ready to fight the brush.

Jodie sighed. "Come on, Felix, you have to let me groom you – otherwise we'll *both* be in trouble!"

Just then, the vacuum cleaner stopped again, and Mrs Taylor called from the bathroom. "Jodie, leave that kitten alone for a moment and come in here, will you?"

Jodie put the brush down on the bed and went out to her mum. Felix pounced on the blue creature, biting and kicking it. "Caught you!" he growled happily.

"Have you had Felix in here with you?" Jodie's mum asked sternly when Jodie went into the bathroom.

Jodie nodded. "He likes to sit and watch me clean my teeth."

"I thought so," Mrs Taylor said, "because there are hairs in the sink *and* on the flannels." Mrs Taylor shook her head. "Wherever I look there's a smudge of grey fluff!"

"But what can I do, Mum?" Jodie said. "Felix can't help moulting."

"I never seem to stop cleaning these days," Mrs Taylor grumbled. "Not since Felix arrived." And then she stared at a toothbrush in horror. "That's the limit!" she cried. "There's cat hair on my toothbrush!"

"Perhaps the special comb we've

ordered from the pet shop will work," Jodie said.

Her mum nodded. "I hope so – I feel quite worn out with all the extra work."

Feeling guilty, Jodie escaped back to her bedroom and watched as Felix burrowed under her duvet again, leaving a cloud of grey fluff behind him. She just hoped that Felix would allow her to use the new comb on him. If he didn't, she could see things getting *very* difficult . . .

Chapter Four

A couple of days later, Jodie and her mum made their way to Pearce's Perfect Pets after school. Mr Pearce had called to say the special comb was in.

As they approached the pet shop Jodie noticed that Felix's photograph was now in the window. "Oh, look, Mum!" she pointed. "There's Felix!

Doesn't he look gorgeous?"

They both stopped and stared at the big photograph of Felix in the middle of the window display. He was wearing his new collar, with his head on one side, looking his cutest. A slogan above the picture read:

Posh Pets
come to
PEARCE'S

Mrs Taylor nodded. "Yes, he looks lovely." Then she gave a little sigh. "But sometimes I can't help wishing that you'd chosen one of the short-haired kittens."

"Don't say that, Mum!" Jodie protested. "I love Felix. He's the most beautiful kitten in the world!"

"He's certainly the fluffiest!" said Mrs Taylor, And then she smiled. "He *is*

gorgeous, and I'm awfully fond of him. But he makes such a lot of mess!"

As they went into the shop, Jodie looked once more at the beautiful photograph of Felix. Who would have thought that choosing the fluffiest kitten would cause such a lot of problems?

"I *wish* you'd let me comb you, Felix!" Jodie said. "It might help with all the fluff, you know."

"Purreow!" Felix said. "I've decided I don't like those things called brushes and combs – they mess up my lovely fur."

Jodie had tried the special comb

for long-haired cats for the first time yesterday. But it hadn't been a great success. Felix treated it just like the blue hairbrush.

As he rolled on the carpet, showing his soft fluffy tummy, Jodie put her hand out for the comb. Half-hiding it in her hand, she very gently combed down his tummy with it and collected some soft fluff in its plastic teeth.

Felix sprang to life. *That* thing again! "Miaow!" He jumped on it, caught it and gave it a good old bite.

"Oh, *Felix*!" Jodie cried, pulling the comb away from him. It already had tiny teeth marks in the handle, where

Felix had attacked it yesterday His kitten teeth were sharp as needles.

"Oh, don't you want to play, then?" Felix miaowed.

Jodie sighed as she heard the monster

cleaner roaring away downstairs again. "Maybe you'll let me groom you when you get older," she said.

Felix stared up at her with his bright blue eyes. No, he didn't think so . . .

Just then, the doorbell rang downstairs and the vacuum cleaner was hastily switched off. As Mrs Taylor opened the door, Jodie could hear a very familiar voice. Then her mum called upstairs.

"Jodie! Mrs Oberon's here. Come and say hello!"

Jodie gathered Felix up. "Mrs Oberon is organising the school fête this year," she told him. "She's my teacher. She's a bit posh and strict – but quite nice really."

"Of course I'd be delighted to help at the school fête," Mrs Taylor was saying, as Jodie carried Felix into the sitting room. "Just let me know what you'd like me to do."

The smartly dressed visitor was sitting on the sofa. "Oh thank you!" she said. Then she smiled at Jodie. "Hello, Jodie – lovely kitten!" she added, seeing Felix. "Maybe we should have a cat competition at the fête. He'd be bound to win!"

Felix purred with pleasure. He liked Mrs Oberon.

Jodie and her mum showed Mrs Oberon to the door, then waited until their guest had reached the front gate.

Suddenly, Mrs Taylor gasped. "Oh no!"

"What?" Jodie asked, puzzled.

"Mrs Oberon's skirt!" Mrs Taylor whispered.

"What about it?" Jodie asked, even more puzzled. She hadn't noticed anything strange about it.

"Didn't you see?" said her mum, closing the door. "All down the back of it – grey fluff!"

Jodie went into the sitting room to look at the sofa. There was fluff all over the cushions again. She hurriedly tried to brush it off.

"I thought I told you not to let that kitten on the sofa!" Mrs Taylor thundered.

Felix, who was still sitting on the sofa, took one look at Mrs Taylor's angry face and disappeared underneath it.

"This is so embarrassing!" Jodie's mum went on. "What on earth will Mrs Oberon think when she gets home and sees her skirt covered in fluff?" Jodie didn't really think there was anything wrong with having cat fluff on your skirt. Or on the carpet or the sofa, or in the bath. But her mum sighed heavily. "This is the last straw! I'm beginning to think that kitten of yours ought to live in the garage, you know."

"Mum!" Jodie protested. "We can't do that – he'd hate it!"

Felix, lying flat underneath the sofa, gave a frightened squeak. This was going too far! A kitten – a *super*kitten like him – couldn't possibly live in a *garage*.

"Well, I just can't think of another solution," Mrs Taylor said. "He refuses to be groomed, he won't stay off the furniture . . . and all I do is clean the place morning, noon and night!"

"But, Mum—" Jodie was just about to start pleading with her mum when the phone rang.

"Bill Pearce here, lass," a voice said when Jodie answered it. "From Pearce's Perfect Pets. How's your fluffy kitten?"

"Er . . . he's OK," Jodie said, looking at her mum, who was still frowning and was about to start vacuuming again.

"And did the new comb do the trick?"
Mr Pearce asked.

"Not exactly," Jodie said uncomfortably.

"Well, it's about that – about the fluff – that I'm ringing you," Mr Pearce went on. "Can I have a word with your mum?"

Jodie handed the phone to Mrs Taylor, who spoke with Mr Pearce for a while.

Then she put the phone down, looking puzzled. "Mr Pearce says that he has some people in his shop who want to meet Felix," she said.

Hearing his name, Felix gave a mew of alarm and crawled to the very

back of the sofa. What was happening *now*?

"What's it about, Mum?" Jodie asked, surprised.

"He wouldn't say," Mrs Taylor replied. "But they're coming round straight away." She switched on the vacuum cleaner. "It all sounds most mysterious."

Chapter Five

"Hello," Jodie said shyly, as Mr Pearce brought a small, smiling man and a tall woman with frizzy red hair into the house.

"This is Mr Tomkins and his assistant, Miss Spark," said Mr Pearce.

"Pleased to meet you," said Jodie's mum, shaking hands with them.

"Although I can't think why you wanted to meet Felix."

Felix was watching from underneath the sofa. What did these people want with him?

"If I may explain," Mr Tomkins said, stepping forward. "My assistant, Miss Spark here, visited Mr Pearce's shop a few days ago and admired the photograph of Felix in the window . . ."

Felix, with a soft miaow, came out from under the sofa. "Here I am!"

The two visitors gave an "Aaah!" of admiration.

"Oh, how sweet!" Miss Spark cried. Her red curls bobbed round her pointy

50

face. "Mr Pearce told me that Felix was the fluffiest kitten he'd ever seen!" she said.

"And I'm pleased to see he's very fluffy indeed," Mr Tomkins added.

Jodie picked up Felix and stroked him proudly. A small shower of grey fluff floated out from his coat. Everyone watched as it slowly sank to the floor. Jodie's heart sank too. Was her mum going to be angry?

"Ahem . . ." said Miss Spark. "Mr Pearce also told me you were having a spot of trouble with Felix's fluff."

"Well, yes," said Mrs Taylor. She glanced at Jodie. "It's true that all I seem to do these days is clean up after Felix. I've got a vacuum cleaner but it's not really up to the job."

"And that is why we're here!" boomed Mr Tomkins happily.

"Shall I go and get it, sir?" Miss Spark asked, a hint of excitement in her voice.

Mr Tomkins nodded. "If you don't mind, Miss Spark."

Miss Spark went to the white van parked outside. She came back in carrying a strange, shiny machine. Written on the side, in bright blue letters, was *Wizard*.

"It looks like a robot!" Jodie said, staring at the large silver box with arms attached.

Felix jumped down from Jodie's arms and approached the machine. What a strange-looking creature! He saw himself in the shiny surface. "Miiaoww!" What a fine-looking kitten!

"This," said Mr Tomkins proudly, "is my latest invention. It's not *just* a vacuum cleaner . . ."

Felix backed away from the silver creature. "Is *that* a vacuum cleaner?" he miaowed.

". . . It's *the* vacuum cleaner!" Mr Tomkins continued. "Better than any other!" He beamed at Jodie and her mum. "I've called it the Wizard because it can clean any house like magic!"

"Really?" Mrs Taylor looked at it

wistfully. "Well, it looks very good, but—"

Mr Tomkins held up his hand. "Please allow us to demonstrate . . ." He turned to his assistant. "Miss Spark, would you plug in the Wizard, please?"

"Certainly, Mr Tomkins," his assistant replied. By now, Miss Spark's red curls seemed to fizz with excitement.

Felix wondered if he should make a dash for it. He'd heard the dreaded words "vacuum cleaner", and that usually meant trouble.

But while he was deciding, Miss Spark switched the machine on. The silver creature began to hum.

Felix sat with his head on one side and stared, puzzled. Why wasn't it making a nasty loud roaring sound like Mrs Taylor's vacuum cleaner?

Miss Spark began to put the machine through its paces, moving one of its long rubbery arms over the sofa.

"Look at that!" Mrs Taylor cried, delighted. The sofa cushions looked brand new!

Then Miss Spark pushed the machine across the carpet. "With one gentle push, the Wizard slides easily along the floor, picking up every single hair as it passes," she said.

"It picks up fluff you didn't know you had!" Mr Tomkins joked.

Felix watched the humming silver creature gliding smoothly along the carpet. It didn't seem fierce, like the other vacuum cleaner. And he did like being able to see himself in the creature's shiny body. Perhaps he should make friends with it.

Felix ran towards the machine, jumped on it and pawed at his reflection.

"Felix looks as if he's driving it!" Jodie laughed.

Everyone smiled, watching Felix as he sat on the Wizard like a figurehead.

His purring was almost as loud as the Wizard's hum.

As Miss Spark steered the Wizard past Jodie, Felix looked up. "Hey, Jodie!" he miaowed. "This is fun!"

Mrs Taylor shook her head in awe, looking at the spotless sofa and carpet. "I've never seen the place looking so clean," she said. "At least, not since Felix has been here."

Jodie had to agree.

"And finally," said Miss Spark as she switched the vacuum cleaner off, "the Wizard also sucks fluff and dust from the air – before it has a chance to settle."

"That's fantastic!" Jodie said.

As the machine stopped moving, Felix stepped off and sat next to his new friend, his head on one side.

Mr Pearce began clapping. "It looks as though Felix thinks he's done the cleaning himself," he said.

"He's an absolute darling!" Miss Spark cried.

Felix was really enjoying himself. Everyone seemed to think he was great! And now that his silver friend had cleaned up all his fluff, perhaps Mrs Taylor would forget about banishing him to the garage.

But Jodie's mum was looking worried again. "It's a marvellous machine," she said. "I'd love one – but I'm afraid we simply can't afford a new vacuum cleaner. Especially such an expensive-looking one . . ."

"Oh, I don't want you to *buy* one!" Mr Tomkins said.

Chapter Six

"What?" Mrs Taylor said in surprise.

"Let me explain," said Mr Tomkins. "We want Felix to star in our advertisements," he said.

Jodie gasped.

"He's a natural," Mr Tomkins went on. "With Felix showing off the Wizard, we'll sell thousands!"

"Oh, wow!" Jodie cried. She picked up Felix and hugged him. "You're going to be famous!" she whispered.

Felix rubbed his head against Jodie's neck. "Great!" he purred. "I've always wanted to be a superkitten."

"I can see the posters now," Mr Tomkins said, rubbing his hands together happily. "They'll say: *Buy a Wizard – the ultimate fluffbuster!*"

"Or how about: *So quiet it won't even frighten a kitten!*" Miss Spark added.

"Very good, Miss Spark!" Mr Tomkins boomed.

"And: *So light even a kitten can push it!*" Mr Pearce offered. "If you don't mind me joining in," he added, going a bit red.

"Thank you, Mr Pearce! Another excellent suggestion!" cried Mr Tomkins. Then he turned to Jodie's mum. "We'll

pay a fee, of course. And the 'Wizard Kitten' must have a Wizard for his own home. We'll leave this one for you, shall we?"

Jodie and her mum stood there, too astounded to speak. Felix gave a short miaow. "Say yes!" He wanted to be a superkitten. He wanted to be famous – and he wanted it now!

One evening, a few weeks later, Jodie and her mum and dad were all sitting in front of the television. Felix was sitting on Jodie's lap. He was quite a bit bigger, but still very fluffy.

"Mr Tomkins said it would be on at

five-thirty," Jodie said. She looked at her watch. "It's nearly that now."

"I only make it twenty-five past," Mr Taylor said.

Felix looked up at Jodie, his bright blue eyes puzzled. Why was everyone so excited? Even Jodie's dad had come home from work early

"Have we got the video set?" Mrs Taylor asked.

Just then there was a noise outside in the hall and a cheerful woman put her head around the door. It was Mrs Bell.

Felix turned round and miaowed. "Hello, Mrs Bell." He liked Mrs Bell.

Ever since Mr Tomkins had paid a lot of money for Felix's kitten modelling, Mrs Bell had been coming here to do all the cleaning.

"I've finished cleaning upstairs," Mrs Bell said. "Do you want me to do in here now?"

"Oh, Mrs Bell," said Jodie's mum, smiling. "Come and watch the advertisement first! It should be on any min—"

She was interrupted by a scream from Jodie. "Here he is! Oh, look, Felix, there you are!"

Jodie held Felix up in front of the television and he saw himself sitting

67

proudly on a Wizard as it was put through its paces.

"Solve even the fluffiest problem with the aid of your Wizard!*"* said a voice on the TV. *"Cleans your home like magic!"*

"Don't you look gorgeous!" Jodie cried.

"Purreow!" said Felix. He jumped down and sat as close to the TV as he could, staring up at himself. "Yes, I do look pretty good . . ."

As the advertisement ended, everyone sighed with pride. Then Felix gave a tiny sneeze and shook himself, sending a shower of fluffy grey fur into the air.

Jodie laughed. "You can do that

as much as you like, Felix," she said.

"Because now you're getting paid for it!"

Snuggles
the Sleepy Kitten

Special thanks to Narinder Dhami
To Vicky's Tigger

Chapter One

Super-Snuggles the Wonder Cat stood very still. His back was arched, and the tip of his tail waved slowly from side to side. Timmy, the biggest fiercest tomcat in town, was walking towards him.

Super-Snuggles stared the ginger tom right in the eyes. One of them would have to move out of the way. Who would it be?

Timmy got closer. And closer . . .

But Super-Snuggles stood his ground. It was about time Timmy treated Super-Snuggles the Wonder Cat with a bit of respect!

"Morning, Super-Snuggles," Timmy miaowed politely. He stepped quickly around the other cat. "And how are you today?"

"Fine," Super-Snuggles purred. "Just fine!"

"Snuggles . . ."

The voice was coming from a long way off.

"Snuggles!"

Snuggles, the tabby kitten, opened one blue eye. His owner, Mr Chapman, was stroking his back.

"Goodness, Snuggles, you've been asleep for hours!" Mr Chapman said. "I was beginning to get worried about you."

"I'm OK, Mr Chapman," Snuggles purred. He yawned and stretched, then rubbed his face against Mr Chapman's cardigan. "In fact, I was having a brilliant dream!"

Snuggles *loved* curling up on Mr Chapman's comfy lap and going to sleep. In his dreams he became Super-Snuggles the Wonder Cat . . .

Super-Snuggles could jump high and run fast. All the other cats in town wanted to be like him. And all the dogs were scared of him. Super-Snuggles could do anything! He could do all the things that Snuggles the kitten was too scared to do.

But Snuggles knew that Mr Chapman

worried about him, because he slept so much.

"I can't become Super-Snuggles the Wonder Cat *unless* I'm asleep!" Snuggles purred, looking up into his owner's kind old face. "I wish I could make you understand."

"Don't go to sleep again, Snuggles," Mr Chapman said anxiously. "Why don't you go and play in the garden for a while?"

Snuggles stopped purring. "The garden!" he mewed worriedly. "What if Timmy the tomcat chases me?" Snuggles was very scared of bad-tempered Timmy – except in his dreams!

"Come on, Snuggles." Mr Chapman picked the kitten up and carried him into the kitchen. "I'll come with you."

Snuggles couldn't help shivering as his owner unlocked the back door. The outside world seemed such a scary place.

Mr Chapman put Snuggles down on the lawn. The kitten padded slowly across the grass, looking around him worriedly as he went.

Suddenly, Snuggles noticed a small hole in the bottom of the fence. His whiskers twitched with interest. The house on the other side had been empty for as long as Snuggles had lived with Mr Chapman. Snuggles had heard his owner say that its garden had become very overgrown – like a jungle! Snuggles imagined it to be a very frightening place.

But even though he was scared, the kitten couldn't resist having a quick peep through the hole. He poked his stripy face through and . . .

WHAT WAS THAT?

Something was moving in there!

Snuggles dashed into the house as fast as his paws could carry him.

"Snuggles, it's only a blackbird!" Mr Chapman called, as he saw what had frightened his kitten. The bird flew up over the fence and into a tree.

But Snuggles had had enough of the big scary world outside.

Mr Chapman came back in, shaking his head. As soon as he sat down, Snuggles jumped onto his owner's lap and curled up in a tight little ball. It was the only place he felt safe.

"No, Snuggles, don't go to sleep again," Mr Chapman said. "Wake up!"

But Snuggles was already fast asleep.

Chapter Two

"I don't think there's anything to worry about, Mr Chapman," said the vet. She finished examining Snuggles. "He seems fine."

"Of *course* I'm fine," Snuggles mewed, as Mr Chapman put him back into his basket. "I could have told you that!" While his owner was talking to the vet, the kitten snuggled into his blanket and closed his eyes.

By the time they left the surgery, Snuggles was fast asleep . . .

Super-Snuggles the Wonder Cat was prowling round Mr Chapman's back garden. One flick of his tail, and not a single bird even *dared* to land in any of the trees.

Super-Snuggles stared at the fence in between Mr Chapman's garden and the one next door. "I wonder what the other garden's like?" he miaowed to himself.

The fence was very high, but that wasn't a problem for Super-Snuggles the Wonder Cat.

"Here I go!" Super-Snuggles miaowed loudly. He sprang into the air, soared over the fence – and landed safely on the other side. "That was easy!" he purred.

Super-Snuggles looked around the garden. There were lots of tall trees to climb. But best of all, there was a large pond, filled with plump, orange fish . . .

"Snuggles?"

Mr Chapman's voice suddenly popped into the kitten's dream.

"Not now," Super-Snuggles mewed crossly. "I want to explore next door's garden."

"Snuggles, wake up!"

Crossly, Snuggles opened an eye. He didn't *want* to wake up. His dream was too exciting!

"We're home, Snuggles," said Mr Chapman. "And look, a new family is moving in next door."

Snuggles stretched, then sat up in his travelling basket. An enormous lorry was parked in the road. Four men were lifting furniture out of it. A woman was standing in next door's garden with a boy. She had a toddler in her arms – a little girl.

The woman waved at Mr Chapman. "Hello, we're your new neighbours!" she called. "I'm Sue Bourne, and these are my children, Mark and Emily."

"Hello," Mr Chapman called back. "I'm Ron Chapman. And this is my kitten Snuggles." He held up the cat basket.

Snuggles looked at the new people, feeling a bit nervous. They *seemed* friendly, he thought.

"Oh, I love cats!" said Mark. He

86

hurried over to get a closer look at Snuggles. "Hello," he said. He reached through the bars of the basket to tickle Snuggles's head.

"Hello," Snuggles purred back.

"Do you have a cat, Mark?" Mr Chapman asked.

Mark shook his head. "No. But I used to go to my best friend Paul's house and play with his kitten after school. And Mum and Dad have said I can have my own cat when Emily's a bit older," he added eagerly.

"Pussy-cat!" said Emily. She leaned over and tried to grab Snuggles's basket.

"Well, Mark, you're welcome to come

and play with Snuggles," Mr Chapman said, smiling.

Mark's face lit up. "Thanks, Mr Chapman."

Snuggles was pleased too. Mark seemed very friendly.

"And you must come and have tea with us, when we've settled in," Mrs Bourne said to Mr Chapman.

"Can Snuggles come too, Mum?" Mark asked quickly.

"Of course!" his mum agreed.

CRASH!

Snuggles almost leaped out of his basket as one of the removal men dropped a box onto the pavement. He wriggled under his blanket and lay there out of sight, shaking with fear.

"Oh dear!" Mrs Bourne groaned. "Well, it was nice to meet you, Mr Chapman." She hurried out of the garden to inspect the box.

"And nice to meet you too, Snuggles!" Mark added.

Snuggles gingerly poked his head out to mew goodbye.

"Well, the Bournes seem very friendly, don't they, Snuggles?" Mr Chapman remarked. He carried Snuggles into the house, then let him out of his basket. "It'll be nice to have someone living next door again."

But Snuggles wasn't listening. He trotted into the living room and curled up on the rug.

By the time Mr Chapman had made himself a cup of tea, the kitten was fast asleep again. "Oh, *Snuggles*!" Mr Chapman sighed. "What *am* I going to do with you?"

Chapter Three

"And you be careful with those boxes!" Super-Snuggles the Wonder Cat miaowed. He kept a stern eye on the removal men going in and out of the house next door. "They belong to my friend Mark, and I'll be very cross if you drop them!"

The removal men were carrying the

boxes very slowly and carefully into the house.

"Good!" Super-Snuggles purred. "Just remember that I'm watching you . . ."

"Snuggles, you'll have to get off my lap."

Snuggles opened his eyes to find Mr Chapman gently lifting him up.

"There's someone at the door," Mr Chapman went on, putting the kitten down on the carpet.

Snuggles yawned. "I was having a brilliant dream," he mewed sleepily. "I really made those removal men behave themselves!"

Mr Chapman went to answer the door.

Snuggles padded after him, and saw their new neighbour standing on the doorstep. "Hello, Mark!" he purred happily.

"Hello, Mr Chapman," Mark said. "We were wondering if you and Snuggles would like to come round and have tea with us."

"Well, that's very kind of you," Mr Chapman said, looking very pleased.

Mark beamed. "Can I carry Snuggles over to my house, please?" he asked hopefully.

Mr Chapman nodded. So Mark carefully scooped the kitten into his arms.

Snuggles cuddled nervously against his new friend. He didn't really like going outside the house.

As they walked down Mr Chapman's path, a dog in one of the nearby houses began to bark loudly.

Snuggles stiffened in alarm. "Uh-oh!" he hissed. "It's big Barney! I've seen him walk past our garden – he's really fierce!" He tried to scramble down the neck of Mark's sweatshirt.

"That's Barney the Alsatian," Mr Chapman explained to Mark. "He belongs to Mr Gordon at Number 21. I'm afraid Snuggles is a bit scared of him."

"No, I'm not!" Snuggles mewed indignantly. "Well, maybe just a tiny bit . . ."

When they were safely inside Mark's house, Snuggles felt much happier. He looked around curiously. All the furniture was in place now, but there were still lots of cardboard boxes to be unpacked.

"Let's play in the garden, Snuggles," Mark suggested. "We've got time before tea."

"The *garden*?" Snuggles mewed, his eyes wide. Go into that scary, dark, overgrown garden? He wasn't sure he liked that idea very much . . .

Mark unlocked the back door and carried Snuggles outside. He gently put the kitten down on the path, then ran off down the overgrown lawn. "Come on, Snuggles!" he called, taking a small rubber ball from his pocket. "Bet you can't get to the ball before I do!" He threw the ball across the garden.

"I bet I can!" Snuggles miaowed. Without thinking, he raced into the grass – which was almost as tall as he was. He found the ball and pounced down on top of it, so that it was hidden under his fat, furry little tummy.

Mark laughed. "That's cheating, Snuggles!"

"Oh, all right," Snuggles mewed, and stood up. But when Mark bent down to pick the ball up, Snuggles batted it smartly with his paw. The ball rolled away across the grass, out of Mark's reach.

"Snuggles, stop it!" Mark laughed. This time he grabbed the ball before the kitten reached it, and threw it across the lawn again.

Snuggles rushed after the ball so quickly he did a somersault, and landed SPLAT! on his bottom.

"Oh, Snuggles, you're so funny!" Mark grinned.

"Maybe, but I've got the ball!" Snuggles purred, batting it away from Mark again with his paw.

Snuggles was quite amazed. The garden wasn't as scary as he'd thought! It *was* a bit dark and overgrown, but he didn't feel frightened – because Mark was playing in it too.

Mark took Snuggles to explore the wild patch at the bottom of the garden. They hid behind trees and jumped out at each other. They even rolled around in a big pile of grass cuttings. Then Mark fetched some empty cardboard boxes. He built a big tower and helped Snuggles to climb all the way to the top.

Snuggles really enjoyed playing with his new friend. But after a while he began to feel a bit strange – as though he had forgotten something important . . .

Then he remembered. "Oh!" he mewed. "My afternoon nap!"

The kitten began to make his way back up the garden, towards the house.

"Snuggles?" Mark called, puzzled. "What's the matter?"

"I almost forgot to have my afternoon Super-Snuggles adventure!" Snuggles mewed. He went through the open back door and into the Bournes' living room.

Mr Chapman was sitting on the sofa, talking to Emily, who was in her playpen. Mrs Bourne was laying out cups and plates for tea.

Snuggles leaped up onto his owner's lap, then settled down and closed his eyes.

"I see what you mean about Snuggles sleeping a lot, Mr Chapman!" Mark's mum said, smiling.

Mr Chapman sighed as he stroked his kitten's head.

"Where's Snuggles?" Mark asked, coming into the living room. "Oh!"

Snuggles was almost asleep by now, but he could hear that Mark sounded a bit disappointed.

"We were having a great game," Mark went on.

Yes, we were, thought Snuggles sleepily. He liked playing with Mark. In fact, playing with Mark was *almost* as much fun as a Super-Snuggles dream . . .

Chapter Four

Super-Snuggles stood outside Number 21, his tail waving angrily from side to side. Inside the house, a dog was barking loudly

"That Barney!" Super-Snuggles hissed crossly. "He's always barking. It's time someone sorted him out!"

The garden gate was shut. It was

quite high, but that didn't stop Super-Snuggles. He leaped over it, and strolled up the garden path. The front door of Number 21 was shut, but a window at the side of the house was open. Super-Snuggles jumped onto the windowsill and looked inside.

Barney the Alsatian was standing in the kitchen. "In case anyone has forgotten, I'M in charge around here," he barked. "This is MY—" Barney stopped when he saw Super-Snuggles glaring at him through the window. "Er . . . hello, Super-Snuggles," he woofed – *much* more quietly. "Is something wrong?"

"There certainly is," Super-Snuggles

miaowed coolly. He stepped through the window and onto the draining board, his whiskers twitching.

Barney looked a bit nervous. "What?" he woofed.

"There's an annoying dog in my street who never stops barking!" Super-Snuggles hissed, staring hard at Barney.

The big dog bared his teeth.

"Grr! You tell me who's annoying you, Super-Snuggles, and I'll see him off!" he growled.

Really! Super-Snuggles thought. *Dogs are so stupid!* "The dog's name is Barney, and he lives at Number 21," he miaowed.

"Right!" Barney barked. Then he

looked puzzled. "Hang on a minute, that's *me*, isn't it?"

Super-Snuggles jumped down onto the kitchen floor, stalked over to the Alsatian and looked him in the eye. "Yes, it is," he miaowed.

Barney's ears and tail drooped. "Sorry. I'll never bark loudly again, Super-Snuggles!" he whimpered. "I promise . . ."

"That's Mark at the door!"

Hearing this, Snuggles left Super-Snuggles telling Barney off, and woke up. He jumped off Mr Chapman's lap and raced down the hall.

It was a few days since Snuggles and

Mr Chapman had gone to tea at the Bournes' house. And Mark had called in to play with the kitten every afternoon when he got home from school.

Snuggles really enjoyed the lively games they played. Kind old Mr Chapman had the comfiest lap in the world, but he couldn't run around the garden with Snuggles like Mark did.

"Hello, Mark," Snuggles purred, as Mr Chapman opened the door. The kitten launched himself at Mark and pounced on the laces of his trainers. It was one of his favourite games.

"Hi, Mr Chapman," Mark grinned. "Can I have my laces back, please,

Snuggles? I need them to keep my trainers on!"

"Why?" Snuggles grabbed one of the laces in his teeth and shook it from side to side. "I don't know why people wear such smelly shoes anyway!"

"Snuggles, behave yourself!" Mr Chapman laughed. "Come in, Mark."

"Race you to the back door, Mark!" Snuggles miaowed happily. And he shot off down the hall, with Mark chasing after him.

When Mr Chapman had unlocked the back door, Snuggles and Mark ran out into the garden. Snuggles had almost forgotten that he'd ever been scared of

going outside. Now he and Mark went out whenever the weather was fine.

It was a crisp, bright autumn day. Red and gold leaves were falling gently from the trees onto the lawn.

"Come on, Mark!" Snuggles mewed. "Let's catch the leaves for a while!" He jumped up at a leaf as it floated down towards him and batted it with his paw.

"Well done, Snuggles!" Mark called. Then he looked around the garden. "I feel like climbing a tree," he said.

Snuggles's heart sank. "I'm too scared to climb trees," he mewed quietly. "Only Super-Snuggles can do that."

Mark pointed at the tallest tree in Mr Chapman's garden. "Come on, Snuggles. Let's climb that one!"

Snuggles looked nervously at the tree. It was so tall, it seemed to go on for ever. Even Super-Snuggles hadn't climbed it yet. Snuggles was sure *he'd* never be able to climb the tree. Not even with Mark's help.

"I'll give you a hand, Snuggles." Mark picked up the kitten and, standing on tiptoe, placed him on one of the lower branches. "Now just wait there while I climb up to you."

"I'm not going anywhere!" Snuggles mewed in a scared voice. "Help!" The kitten was very frightened indeed. He felt as though he was going to fall off any minute. He didn't like it at all.

"Mark, your mum's here," Mr Chapman called from the back door. Snuggles was *very* relieved.

"OK," Mark called back. He lifted

Snuggles off the branch. "The tree will have to wait until tomorrow," he said. Then he gave the kitten a cuddle as he carried him back into the house.

Snuggles was still feeling a bit shaky, so he decided to go and have a nap. A Super-Snuggles adventure would make him feel better.

Mr Chapman was busy in the kitchen, so the kitten curled up on the rug in front of the fire. What would Super-Snuggles do today? he wondered. He'd have to wait and see . . .

*

Super-Snuggles the Wonder Cat sat on the front garden fence, watching all the dogs in the street walking up and down. They hardly made a sound.

"Hello, Super-Snuggles," Barney woofed very softly, trotting up to him. "I've told all the other dogs not to bark loudly any more, because it annoys you."

"Thanks, Barney," Super-Snuggles miaowed.

The Alsatian wagged his tail happily.

Super-Snuggles sat and watched all the dogs woofing to each other really, really quietly. It was great fun!

Or was it?

"Just a minute," Super-Snuggles mewed, feeling rather miserable. "Something's not quite right here . . ."

Snuggles stirred in his sleep, beginning to wake up. *What is the matter with Super-Snuggles?* he thought drowsily. *Why does he feel so fed up?*

"Snuggles, wake up." Mr Chapman came into the living room carrying a sandwich and a cup of tea. "Were you asleep again? I sometimes wonder what you dream about!"

"Oh, I always have *great* dreams, Mr Chapman," Snuggles miaowed, yawning. "Being Super-Snuggles the Wonder Cat is the most fun ever!" But then he sat up and thought hard. His dream hadn't felt quite so exciting today.

Snuggles felt a bit upset. He could hardly eat any of the tuna that Mr Chapman offered him.

What was the matter with him? He always *loved* being Super-Snuggles in his dreams. So why hadn't he enjoyed *this* dream? What had changed?

The kitten decided to go back to sleep. Maybe he could find out.

Chapter Five

Super-Snuggles bounded over the fences into every garden in the street. At Number 21, Barney was waiting for him.

"Hello, Super-Snuggles," Barney woofed quietly. "Welcome to my garden. I've got a big fish for you from my owner's fridge."

"Thanks." Super-Snuggles ate the fish and then leaped over the fence into the next garden.

Mrs Foster's Boxer, Jason, was sitting there with a whole roast chicken in front of him. "I hope you like it, Super-Snuggles," he woofed politely.

"It will do," Super-Snuggles miaowed. And he ate the whole lot. Then he jumped over two more fences into the garden of Number 27, where Mr Lane's mongrel, Sally, had a pork chop waiting for him.

"You're my hero, Super-Snuggles," Sally woofed, wagging her tail at him.

"Hang on a minute." Super-Snuggles

sat down. "Something's not right here," he mewed miserably.

"Oh no! It's happening again!" Snuggles miaowed as he woke up. It had been a great dream – all the scary dogs in the street giving Super-Snuggles his favourite food!

But Super-Snuggles just wasn't enjoying himself any more. And Snuggles didn't know why.

"Snuggles, what's wrong?" Mr Chapman put down his newspaper and gently scratched the kitten's head. "You don't look very happy."

"I'm not!" Snuggles mewed miserably. No matter what Super-Snuggles did, the dreams weren't so exciting. They didn't feel very *real*.

But Snuggles was determined not to give up. "Maybe I should sleep even *more*," he mewed. "Then I might be able to get my lovely, exciting dreams back!"

Snuggles thought that this was a

really good idea. So he curled up on Mr Chapman's lap again.

"Oh, Snuggles, you're not going to sleep *again*!" Mr Chapman exclaimed. "You've only just woken up!"

Just then the doorbell rang.

"Aren't you coming to see who it is, Snuggles?" Mr Chapman asked. He lifted the kitten off his lap and slowly stood up. "It might be Mark."

"I can't," Snuggles miaowed, keeping his eyes tightly shut. "I *have* to have a really good dream . . ."

"Hi, Mr Chapman."

Snuggles recognised Mark's voice. The kitten longed to rush into the hall and say hello. But he stayed where he was.

"Mum wants to know if you and Snuggles would like to come to lunch today," Mark went on.

"We'd love to," Mr Chapman agreed. "If I can wake Snuggles up, that is!"

"Oh, is he asleep again?" said Mark, coming into the living room.

Snuggles kept his eyes closed and pretended to be asleep, even when Mark crouched down to stroke him.

"Don't you want to play, Snuggles?" Mark sounded very disappointed.

Snuggles felt guilty about not getting

up to play with his friend. But he didn't move.

"Never mind, Mark," said Mr Chapman. "You'll be able to play with Snuggles when we come over for lunch."

"OK," said Mark. But he still sounded upset. "Mum says to come over at about one o'clock." Then he went back next door.

Snuggles felt very mean. He didn't want to make Mark unhappy. He loved Mark nearly as much as he loved Mr Chapman, now.

The kitten decided that he would play with Mark all afternoon to make it up to him. "But now I *must* get to sleep," he sighed.

Super-Snuggles stood looking up at the huge tree. Its branches stretched right up into the sky. It was a long way to the top, but Super-Snuggles knew he could do it.

He began to climb. He leaped lightly from branch to branch, getting higher with every jump. The tree swayed gently in the breeze, but that didn't worry Super-Snuggles the Wonder Cat. He just kept right on going.

"I did it!" Super-Snuggles miaowed, as he jumped up onto the highest branch. "I climbed the tallest tree!"

It should have been one of the best dreams ever.

"But it isn't," Super-Snuggles miaowed sadly. He looked down into next door's garden. Mark was out there, playing with his little sister. He was chasing her round the garden, and they were laughing happily.

"You know what?" Super-Snuggles the Wonder Cat miaowed. "I wish *I* could play with Mark!"

Chapter Six

"OH!" Snuggles woke up with a jolt.

"Snuggles!" Mr Chapman was staring at his kitten, looking puzzled. "You made me jump! What's the matter?"

"It's OK, Mr Chapman," Snuggles mewed. "*Now* I know why my Super-Snuggles adventures aren't such fun any more."

Mr Chapman stared down at his excited little kitten. "What on *earth* is the matter with you, Snuggles?"

"My real world is more exciting than my dream world, now that I've got Mark to play with!" Snuggles explained happily.

He jumped off Mr Chapman's lap, and charged to the front door, tail waving madly. "I'm tired of dreaming. Can we go and see Mark now?"

"Snuggles, what's the matter?" Mr Chapman came out into the hall. "Don't scratch the door!"

"*Please*, Mr Chapman," Snuggles mewed.

Mr Chapman picked up his kitten, then looked at his watch. "Let's go next door," he said. "It's nearly time for lunch. And at least that will stop you scratching my front door to pieces!"

As Mr Chapman carried Snuggles

outside, the kitten's heart thumped with excitement. How could he have thought that silly old dreams could be better than having *real* adventures, playing with Mark?

Mark was looking out for them. His face lit up and he dashed outside to open the front gate.

Mr Chapman handed Snuggles to him.

The kitten rubbed his furry cheek against Mark's. "Sorry, Mark," he purred. "Playing with *you* is the best fun ever!"

"Woof! Woof!"

Snuggles turned round and saw

Barney the Alsatian walking down the street with his owner.

"Grr!" Barney had spotted Snuggles, and was trying to pull his owner towards him. "I don't like cats!" he growled fiercely.

Snuggles's fur bristled in fear. But he couldn't let smelly old Barney spoil his fun with Mark. He knew he had to be brave. What would Super-Snuggles do?

The kitten arched his back and lowered his ears, hoping it made him look fierce. "You'd better not talk to me like that, Barney," he hissed. "Or I'll chase you right up the street!"

Barney was so surprised that he stopped barking at once.

"You showed *him*, Snuggles!" Mark laughed, as he carried the kitten inside.

"Yes, I did, didn't I?" Snuggles purred, rather surprised himself.

There were delicious smells coming from the kitchen which made Snuggles's whiskers twitch.

"Let's go into the garden, Snuggles." Mark put the kitten down, and went to open the back door. "I'll show you my new tree house."

"Great!" Snuggles purred happily.

Mark's tree house was perched in the branches of the tallest tree in the

Bournes' garden. Snuggles could see that the tree was even taller than the one Super-Snuggles had climbed in Mr Chapman's garden. There was a long ladder leading up to the tree house.

"Shall I carry you up there, Snuggles?" Mark asked, bending to pick the kitten up.

"No," Snuggles miaowed bravely. He shrugged away Mark's hand. "I'm going to *climb* up the tree – just like Super-Snuggles would!"

"You'll never get up there!" someone miaowed rudely.

Snuggles turned round and saw

Timmy the tomcat perched on the fence, his tail swinging.

"Oh yes, I will!" Snuggles mewed back. It was funny – he didn't feel scared of Timmy at *all* now!

Mark began to climb up the ladder and Snuggles scrambled up the tree trunk behind him. It wasn't easy and his legs were tired out before he was halfway there. But he kept going.

The sun was warm on the kitten's back. A gentle breeze ruffled his fur. "I did it!" Snuggles miaowed, as he finally reached the tree house.

He could see all the streets and gardens for miles around. He was so

close to the blue sky that he felt as if he could reach out with his paw and touch it.

Snuggles thought that this was better than *any* of his Super-Snuggles dreams. He wasn't scared at all, now that he'd got used to the swaying movements of the tree. But best of all, Mark was there too.

Snuggles and Mark played in the tree house until lunch was ready.

Then Mrs Bourne called them in, and everyone sat down to a huge roast chicken, with lots of potatoes, vegetables and gravy.

Snuggles had his own special bowl under the table, which was full of small pieces of meat. And Mark kept slipping him more bits too! Snuggles had never been so full in his life.

After lunch, Snuggles curled up on Mr Chapman's lap and yawned. He was tired out from all their energetic games and from eating so much food.

"Look, Snuggles is going to sleep again," laughed Mrs Bourne.

"Well, I think he deserves a nap this time," Mr Chapman smiled.

"Yes, he's been awake for ages," agreed Mark.

"Don't worry, Mr Chapman," Snuggles mewed. "I'm not going to sleep for long. As soon as my tummy's not so full, I'm going out with Mark to climb another tree!"

Star
the Snowy Kitten

Special thanks to Mary Hooper
To Maisie – a star in her own right

Chapter One

Michael knelt down beside the fire in his gran's flat and ruffled Archie's fur. The big tabby cat began to purr.

"I wish Archie could come and live with us," Michael said.

"Don't be silly," Mrs Tappin, his mum, replied. "What would Gran do without him?"

Michael put his head down onto Archie's tummy. "I'd love a kitten of my own even more."

His mum and gran looked at each other and raised their eyebrows.

Michael closed his eyes and wished. *I really hope I get a kitten for Christmas.*

It was Christmas Eve and Michael and his mum had just popped in to see his gran. Archie, her cat, was dozing in front of the electric fire.

Archie was old now, with raggedy fur. Once he'd been lean and active, but now he was large and soft, his body sprawled out like a bag of knitting.

"I thought you wanted a mountain

144

bike!" Michael's gran said. Michael opened his eyes. "I'm *saving* for a mountain bike," he replied. "I've been saving for ages. But I'd like a kitten for my Christmas present."

"You got a kitten last Christmas," his mum reminded him.

"But that wasn't a real one," Michael argued.

Because he'd kept on about kittens so much, one of Michael's presents last year had been a toy kitten, with fluffy ginger fur and curly whiskers. He now sat on the shelf above Michael's bed. Sometimes, when no one was looking, Michael gave him a cuddle.

"You're too young to look after a real kitten yourself," Mrs Tappin said.

"I still want one," said Michael. "I'll *always* want one."

"They cost a lot of money, kittens do," said his gran. "There's food and vet's bills."

"And cat baskets and flea collars!" Mrs Tappin put in.

"But Archie doesn't cost you much, does he, Gran?" Michael asked. He stroked the pale fur on Archie's tummy, which was soft as feathers.

"Not now," his gran replied. "He doesn't need a lot of fuss and expense. All he needs now is a laze in front of the fire and a snooze." She smiled. "Like me!"

Michael put his face close to Archie's and touched the tip of the cat's damp, pink nose with his own. Archie's whiskers quivered and one ear twitched slightly. "Did he play a lot when he was younger? Did he do naughty things?" he asked.

"Oh, my goodness, yes," said his gran. "He used to run up these curtains quicker than a rat up a drainpipe!"

"One Christmas he climbed the tree!" Michael's mum put in. She nodded towards the funny old plastic Christmas tree that his gran put up every Christmas. It was a bit bent and a bit bare. But she said she liked it like that.

"That's how it got bent," said his gran.

Michael looked at Archie's crumpled, sleeping face. "Oh, *please* let me have a kitten!"

Michael's mum and gran looked at each other again.

"You'll have enough money for your bike soon," Mrs Tappin said. "Then you won't want to stay in with a kitten."

"I will," said Michael. "I'll have plenty of time left for a kitten."

Michael's gran walked over to the window. "It said on the news that it's going to snow," she said. "We might have a white Christmas this year!"

Michael looked up. "That would be great!" Then he sighed, and leant down to scratch the soft furry folds around Archie's neck. "But not as great as having a kitten," he said quietly to himself.

*

On the way home, it began, very gently, to snow. A few flakes circled the street lights and fluttered to rest on Michael's anorak.

Chapter Two

On Christmas morning, Michael woke up at six o'clock. *Christmas Day*, he thought. *Presents!*

It was still dark but there was a strange glow coming through the curtains. Michael jumped out of bed to have a look. He pulled back the curtain. "Snow!" he breathed.

There was snow everywhere: on the road, in the gardens, along the roofs of the houses opposite.

Michael had never seen so much snow. "Oh, wow!" he said. Part of him wanted to dash out and build a snowman. But then . . . Christmas was waiting!

There, in the shadows by the bottom of his bed, Michael saw his stocking. It was bulging with presents! Full of excitement, Michael dragged it up and tipped everything out onto his bed.

All the parcels were wrapped in silver and gold. Michael tore off the wrapping to find all sorts of goodies. His favourites

152

were a box with a black cat on it and a book about kittens.

Right at the bottom of the stocking, in its toe, Michael found a handful of chocolate coins covered in gold foil. He peeled four of them, crammed them in

his mouth and then pulled on a jumper, ready to race downstairs.

Under the tree in the sitting room, he knew he'd find his big presents. He still hoped that there might . . . just possibly . . . be a kitten.

Downstairs, the sitting room was lit by the same soft glow as Michael's bedroom. Under the tree, parcels of all different shapes, colours and sizes had arrived, as if by magic. But Michael couldn't see a kitten.

For a moment he felt disappointed.

"Michael!" his mum called from upstairs. "We can hear you!"

"Come up and show us your presents!" his dad said.

Michael began to feel a little bit excited again as he looked at the parcels with his name on them. "Coming!" he called back. He picked up as many of his presents as he could carry and made for the door. But just as he was going out of the room, Michael heard a strange noise.

Miaooww!

Michael was so surprised he dropped some of the parcels he was carrying. He put the rest of them down and began to look for where the noise was coming from.

He looked under the sofa, under the table and chairs, and behind the sideboard. But no luck.

He looked behind the bookcase and out in the hall. He still couldn't find anything. Perhaps he'd imagined it.

Miaaowww!

But there it was again! And it was coming from outside . . .

Michael ran over to the curtains and pulled them open. The garden was blanketed with snow.

And there, pressed up against the glass door that led to the back garden, was a small black kitten. A very snowy kitten.

156

"Oh!" Michael cried. He opened the door and scooped up the kitten in his arms. "What are you doing out there in the snow?"

Holding the bedraggled black bundle against the warmth of his jumper, Michael shivered and quickly closed the door. "I wonder who you belong to?" he whispered.

The kitten looked up at Michael with bright green eyes, then mewed.

And to Michael, it seemed she was saying, "I belong to you!"

Chapter Three

Very quietly, Michael crept upstairs to his bedroom. He put the kitten on his bed and covered it with a fold of duvet to keep it warm.

He stroked its soft damp fur, hardly able to believe it. A kitten, waiting for him on Christmas morning!

The kitten was black, except for a

white, star-shaped mark that stretched from nose to chest.

"I'm going to call you Star," Michael decided. He thought the kitten looked like a girl. He tickled her tiny pointed ears. "You're my Christmas Star!"

The kitten began to purr softly, and rubbed a tiny black cheek against Michael's hand.

"Michael, what *are* you doing?" came his dad's voice.

"Almost there!" Michael called back. He didn't dare tell his mum and dad about Star. They might not let him keep her. No, he'd have to hide her for the time being. And then, after Christmas, he'd think about what to do.

Michael bent to kiss Star's soft forehead. "I'll be back as soon as I can, Star," he whispered. "I'll bring you something to eat."

Quietly, Michael left his bedroom and went downstairs to pick up some of his parcels again.

"Happy Christmas!" his mum and dad said as he went into their bedroom. "Let's see your presents."

There were some great things in Michael's parcels – a computer game, a video and two more books from his favourite animal series. There was also a safety lock, a horn and some lights for his bike – and some money from his gran towards buying it!

"So are you pleased, love?" Mrs Tappin asked, smiling.

Michael nodded. "They're all

brilliant!" he said happily. *Especially my secret present,* he thought to himself.

Later that morning, Michael's mum and dad were getting suspicious. Usually Michael spent Christmas morning downstairs, playing with his new toys and watching TV, but today he'd spent a lot of time upstairs in his room.

"Do you feel all right?" Mrs Tappin asked. "One minute you're here, next you're gone! You've hardly looked at your new bike stuff. I don't think you've even opened your books!"

"I feel great!" Michael replied. "I'm

just going upstairs to . . . to write some thank-you letters."

His dad looked at him with astonishment. "Are you *sure* you feel all right, Michael?"

"Course I do!" Michael said, then he ran up to his room and closed the door behind him.

Snuggled in Michael's duvet, Star was snoozing. Earlier, Michael had brought her up a bowl of breakfast cereal, mashed up with lots of milk. She'd eaten every bit; then, with a round, full tummy, she'd fallen fast asleep. Michael was planning to bring her some turkey later.

Suddenly the kitten's eyes opened. Seeing Michael, she began to purr madly.

Michael gently ruffled the fur around her ears. "Are you ready to play, now?" he asked. He trailed a piece of tinsel that he'd picked off the Christmas tree across the duvet.

As she caught sight of it, Star's green eyes opened wide. She leapt to her feet, then crouched, ears pricked, quivering all over as she prepared to pounce. Suddenly she leapt on the moving tinsel, attacking it with tiny paws and teeth.

Michael laughed out loud. Then his face grew more serious. "I don't know

what to do about you going to the loo, Star," he said. "You're going to want to go soon, now you've woken up." He looked around his room thoughtfully. Star put her head to one side, watching his every move. "I think I'd better put some newspaper under the bed and then you can—"

Suddenly, Michael's door opened and his mum stood in the doorway. Her eyes widened as she saw Star. "Where did you . . . Where has that kitten come from?" she gasped.

Michael ran over and scooped up Star. "She was outside!" he said. "This morning, when I got up to open my presents, she was outside in the snow."

"I don't believe it!" Mrs Tappin said faintly. She sat down on the bed. "Clive," she called to Michael's dad, "come quickly!"

Mr Tappin came hurrying in. He too stopped still in the doorway when he saw the kitten in Michael's arms.

"She's mine!" Michael said fiercely. "I wished for a kitten and Star came along!" He held her close. "You will let me keep her, won't you?" he pleaded.

Mrs Tappin sighed. "I'm sorry, love," she said. "She belongs to someone else. Kittens don't just turn up on your doorstep like magic."

"And whoever she belongs to will be missing her," Mr Tappin added. "We'll have to put her outside again so she can go back to her real home. It's only right." Michael hugged Star even tighter.

"Think how you'd feel if you had a kitten and it just disappeared," his mum said gently.

Michael nodded slowly.

"She'll find her way back to where she came from," Michael's dad reassured him. "But you must say goodbye to her now."

When his mum and dad had left the bedroom, Michael put his head down on Star's fluffy tummy. His wish had come true: he'd got a kitten for Christmas. But now she was being taken away . . .

Chapter Four

"Anyone for second helpings?" Mr Tappin asked. The family were sitting at the dining table, eating Christmas lunch.

Michael's granny always came to lunch on Christmas Day, with Archie. She puffed out her cheeks. "No thanks, love, I'm full," she said.

"If I ate anything else I'd go pop!" said Mr Tappin.

"How about you, Michael?" his mum asked.

Michael shook his head, a great lump in his throat. He'd managed to eat some of his Christmas lunch, but he hadn't enjoyed it half as much as he usually did. He was too worried about Star.

After the kitten had been put back out into the snow, she'd hung around the door for a while, miaowing – then she'd disappeared. Michael's mum and dad had said she'd gone home. But Michael wasn't so sure.

171

"So – who's for Christmas pudding?" Mrs Tappin asked next. Mr Tappin groaned. "Or shall we wait a while?" she added hastily.

"Good idea," Michael's gran said as she sank down on the sofa next to Archie.

Suddenly Michael heard a familiar mewing sound. He turned to look over at the glass door. "Look! Star's come back!" he shouted.

Everyone looked towards the garden. Star stood there in the snow, her fur sticking up in damp spikes. She mewed again, then started scratching at the glass.

"So that's the little thing you've been telling me about!" said Michael's gran.

Michael nodded, then looked at his mum, hopefully.

Mrs Tappin stood up. "If we ignore her, I expect she'll go home. Now, does anyone want a mince pie?"

"But, Mum!" Michael pleaded. "She'll be freezing cold out there. It's starting to snow again. The snow will get so deep that it will go right over her head."

"Cats are very sensible . . ." his mum began, and then she looked at Star and hesitated. "Oh, dear," she said. "She does look a bit wet, doesn't she?"

174

"And it is Christmas . . ." said Michael's gran, winking at him.

"Perhaps just for a little while, then," Mrs Tappin agreed. "Until we can find her owners . . ."

Before they could say anything else, Michael was opening the door and lifting the shivering kitten into his arms. "You came back!" he said, holding her close to him and not caring a bit about his Christmas jumper getting wet.

Mrs Tappin went to get an old towel from the kitchen to dry Star.

Archie seemed to sense that there was something going on and woke up from his snooze. Raising his head, he spotted the tiny intruder, jumped down from the sofa and stood at Michael's feet staring up. He gave a loud, loud miaow. Who was this cheeky young thing?

"You can be introduced in a minute," Michael's gran said. "The youngster needs to be dried first."

Mrs Tappin gave Michael the towel and he sat by the fire with Star on his lap. Very gently he patted her wet fur, rubbing under her tummy where she was wettest of all.

As her fur got dry and fluffy, Star curled round and round on Michael's lap, loving all the attention. Purring non-stop, she put out her tongue and began to lick Michael's hand.

"It feels all tickly," he laughed. He was so happy! He'd wanted a cat for ages . . .

While he'd been drying the kitten, the family had been watching, and now they all thought Star was really sweet.

But *someone* didn't think she was very sweet. Archie stood on red alert, ears pricked and eyes wide, watching the stranger's every movement.

Michael's dad told him to put Star down next to the older cat.

"I hope they'll be friends," Michael said anxiously, lowering Star to the floor.

The big tabby cat and the tiny black

kitten stared at each other. Their noses twitched as they sniffed unfamiliar scents and their tails swung slowly from side to side. They were weighing each other up.

Star took a timid step closer to Archie, but Archie immediately gave a low growl of disapproval. He raised his back into a high arch and fluffed up his raggedy fur.

Star shrank away, scared. Michael moved in to pick her up and protect her. He wasn't going to have his little kitten frightened!

"They'll be friends all in good time," said Michael's gran.

"I expect the little thing's hungry,"
Mrs Tappin said. "Maybe she wants her
Christmas lunch."

Michael nodded eagerly. "Oh, yes,

please," he said. "If you give me some turkey, I'll chop it up for her. And can she have some gravy on it?"

His mum laughed. "I suppose you want the gravy warmed up?"

"Yes, please," Michael said.

Mrs Tappin returned with Star's food and gave it to Michael. He put it down in the middle of the floor and sat down right beside her to watch her eat it.

Star munched away, her tiny white teeth flashing and her pink tongue hungrily licking up the gravy.

"Look at her eat!" Mr Tappin said. "Anyone would think she'd never seen a Christmas lunch before."

180

"She hasn't!" Michael said, and then realised that his dad was joking.

Archie had some turkey too, of course, and when both cats had finished their meal they sat by the fire. They didn't look at each other but sat carefully licking round their mouths and smoothing their whiskers with their paws.

"I think they're going to be friends," Michael said. He beamed at his gran. "Archie can be Star's grandad!"

The three grown-ups looked at each other.

"Don't forget, love," his mum said, "Star might not be here for long. She

181

belongs to someone else. You're just borrowing her."

Michael didn't answer. He watched his lovely kitten, not wanting to miss a lick of her paw or a swish of her tail.

When she'd finished washing, Star stretched and yawned widely. Michael thought she was about to fall asleep but she suddenly leapt right over the dozing Archie and made a beeline for Michael's dad. She ran straight up his trousers, across his jumper and round the back of his neck.

Mr Tappin gave a shout of surprise. "She's climbing onto my head!"

Everyone started laughing.

"It looks like you're wearing a furry scarf!" Michael's gran said.

"Aren't kittens fun!" Michael said, happily.

"Yes, they are," said his mum. But then her face turned serious. "But Michael, you must remember that Star isn't really yours."

Michael pretended not to hear her again. Star was his. She *was* . . .

Chapter Five

"Now, what shall we say on this poster?" asked Mr Tappin.

It was three days after Christmas and he and Michael were sitting at his computer. They'd contacted the RSPCA and the local vet to report that they'd found a kitten, and now they were making a poster.

"I don't know," Michael said. He didn't want to be helpful.

"I suppose we should start off by describing her," said his dad. "Black kitten with white star-shaped mark on her chest . . ."

"What if no one claims her?" Michael asked.

"Don't build your hopes up," Mr Tappin replied. "Someone must be really worried about her."

There was a scratching at the door. Michael went over to open it and Star padded into the room. She rubbed her head against his ankle, purring loudly.

Michael picked Star up and took her

to sit with him. The kitten seemed very interested in the computer and leapt from Michael's lap onto the table.

Zedtonimplurr appeared on the screen as she stepped daintily across the computer keyboard.

"Out of the way, naughty puss," said Mr Tappin, laughing.

Star blinked up at him, giving her cutest look. "Mia–oww!"

Michael's dad grinned. "She is a sweet little thing," he said. "I'll miss her when she goes."

"So will I," said Michael, picking her up and hugging her. *Oh, please,* he thought to himself, *please don't let anyone claim her . . .*

That afternoon, Michael and his dad went round the village, putting up the posters:

KITTEN FOUND ON CHRISTMAS DAY

BLACK, WITH WHITE STAR-SHAPED
MARK ON HER CHEST

Please contact: 8 Harshaw Villas

Telephone: 0126 545 593

"I think we only need to put up one or two posters," Michael said.

"No, we'll need a few more than that," said Mr Tappin. "Maybe ten or twelve."

"I'll do them," Michael said quickly. "You can go home."

Mr Tappin shook his head. "I'm not daft!" he said. "You wouldn't put up any at all if I left you to it, because you

189

don't want anyone to find out we've got Star!"

"I would," Michael said. "But I might put them up back to front," he admitted. "Or I might not push the drawing pin in very hard and they might fall off!"

His dad laughed. "That's why I think I'd better be here."

When they'd put up ten posters, including one in the post office, they walked home.

Star was sitting on the kitchen windowsill, looking out. When she saw Michael she began to miaow happily.

Michael walked into the kitchen and

grinned. "I love having her here, don't you?"

"Yes, I do, love," Mr Tappin said. "But I'm sure the person she belongs to will be searching for her. And they'll soon see one of the posters we've put up."

Michael picked up Star and held her

tightly. He just didn't want to think about that.

The phone call came two days later, just as Michael was about to take Star upstairs to bed.

Mr Tappin answered the phone and Michael saw his face grow serious. "I see. Yes, we've got her," he said. "That's right, black, with a white mark on her chest . . ."

Michael began to feel sick.

"Yes, tomorrow morning will be fine," his dad went on. Mr Tappin put down the phone. "That was a Mrs Patel from Dinby Way."

Michael didn't say anything.

His dad shot him a sympathetic glance. "She bought a kitten for her daughter's birthday a couple of weeks before Christmas and it disappeared."

Michael felt like he was going to cry. "No!" he said.

"Mrs Patel said her daughter misses her kitten very much," his dad said quietly.

Michael scooped Star up and ran upstairs to his bedroom. "Star wants to be with me!" he cried as he slammed the door. "They're not having her!"

Chapter Six

"Post, Michael!" his mum called the next morning. "There's something for you from Scotland."

"OK," Michael said gloomily. He and Star were playing with a ping-pong ball, and he kept thinking that this might be the last time they ever played together.

Star put out a velvety paw and swiped

the ball – right between Michael's knees. "Goal!" he laughed. "Clever girl!" He rolled the ball for Star one last time. While she scooted after it, Michael went into the kitchen.

His mum held out an envelope to him, smiling. "It's from Scottish Granny," she said.

Scottish Granny, who lived near Aberdeen, always sent New Year cards and presents instead of Christmas ones. Michael usually got a book token from her.

He took the envelope and looked at his watch. Nearly eleven o'clock! He'd been up since before it was light

195

that morning, playing with Star. This time tomorrow, someone else would be playing with her.

"Aren't you going to open the card?" Mrs Tappin asked.

Michael nodded, slit open the envelope and pulled out a New Year card. But it didn't have a book token with it. Instead, there was a cheque – for fifty pounds!

"Oh!" Michael cried. "The rest of my bike money – all at once!"

His mum smiled. "Granny knew you'd been saving hard and wanted to help," she explained.

Michael put the card and the cheque

down on the kitchen table. He tried to feel excited. But really all he could think about was Star.

He went back into the sitting room. Star was now curled into a black fluffy ball, fast asleep behind the sofa.

Michael crouched down to watch her. Star's whiskers twitched gently as she breathed in and out. She looked so sweet that Michael felt as if he was going to cry.

Just then, he heard a noise on the gravel outside. There was a knock at the door. Star opened her eyes and peered up at him.

Mrs Tappin came into the room.

"That'll be the people for Star," she said gently. She put an arm round Michael's shoulders. "Be brave, love. You've looked after her very well. And perhaps in a year or so, you can have another kitten – a kitten of your own."

Michael shrugged her arm away. "I don't want another kitten!" he said. He was trying really hard not to cry now.

Michael's dad showed Mrs Patel and her daughter Nashi into the room. Michael thought they looked very nice. But he couldn't like them – they were going to take Star away from him.

"She's behind the sofa," he muttered, then turned away and blew his nose. "She's asleep. She likes sleeping there."

Nashi, a small girl with long plaits, crawled behind the sofa.

Michael held his breath.

After a few long seconds, Nashi crawled out again, looking upset. "It's not her!" she said.

Michael felt the tightness and the tears inside him disappear as if by

magic. He let out his breath in a long sigh.

"Are you sure?" Mrs Patel asked.

Nashi nodded sadly. "It's definitely not our Leyla," she said. "Leyla has one white toe, and a bit of white on the end of her tail as well."

Mrs Patel turned to Michael's mum and dad. "Thank you," she said. "We'll try the vet's next. There's a lost kitten there."

"I really hope you find her," Michael said to Nashi.

Nashi smiled. "Thank you," she said. Then she and her mother went off towards the village vet's.

Michael let out a shout of joy. This made Star jump. She sprang to her feet and, before Michael could catch her, ran straight up Mr Tappin's trouser leg and huddled on his right shoulder.

"Ow!" Michael's dad yelled, hopping around. "Her claws are getting sharper! And she's making holes in all my shirts!"

Star scrambled down his front and pounced on his slippers. What fun!

Michael and his mum couldn't stop laughing. As Star skittered across the wooden floor and hid behind a potted plant, Michael felt so happy, he thought he would burst!

"Well!" Mrs Tappin said.

Then there was a long silence.

"So . . ." said Mr Tappin. "What now?" He scratched his head. "No one else seems to be missing a kitten around here. It's a mystery where she came from."

Star seemed to know something was up. She peeped out from behind the plant, looking from one to the other of them.

Michael took a deep breath. "I'd like to spend my bike money," he announced.

"You want to buy your bike now?" his mum said.

"No . . ." Michael said slowly. "I want to spend the money on Star. She needs

injections and a cat basket and a collar and—"

"Yes, that's true," his dad interrupted. "But . . . what about your bike?"

"I still want it," Michael said, "but

that can wait. Mostly I want to look after Star. And I thought that if I bought all her things myself you might . . . let me keep her . . . if no one else claims her."

Michael's mum and dad looked at each other. "What do you think, Clive?" Mrs Tappin asked.

"Well," Mr Tappin said seriously, "having watched Michael with Star, I *do* think he'd look after her properly."

"So do I," Mrs Tappin agreed, smiling. "And no one's claimed her . . . so . . ."

Michael flew over to Star, picked her up and held her tightly. "Did you hear that, Star?" he said. "You can stay here, with us!"

Star began to purr and rubbed her face against Michael's chin.

"Oh, by the way, Michael . . ." Mr Tappin said.

"Yes, Dad?" Michael asked.

"All that money you've got – how would you like to buy me some new trousers and shirts?" his dad joked.

"And if you've got any money left over, I'd like a new set of sitting-room curtains, please," Michael's mum joined in. "Star seems to think curtains are there for her to use as a climbing frame!"

*

As her new family laughed, Star smiled too – though to anyone else it looked like a yawn. Yes, she thought, she'd chosen her new home very well. And here she was going to stay . . .

Nell
the Naughty Kitten

Special thanks to Angie Sage

Chapter One

"Tom quick, look! Nell's doing it again!" yelled Tom Morgan's twin sisters, Jo and Hattie.

Tom ran to the door and stared across the farmyard to the pigpen. A fat, squealing pig was tearing round the pen in a panic. Sitting calmly on the fence was a little stripy ball of fluff.

The ball of fluff was Nell, the new kitten on the farm.

"Oh no!" Tom pulled on his wellingtons and rushed out into the farmyard. Hattie and Jo ran after him.

Nell's favourite game was playing with the short, curly tail of Poppy, their heavily pregnant pig. But Poppy didn't seem to like this game very much.

Tom ran up to the pigpen just as Poppy skidded to a halt and stamped her trotters crossly. Nell jumped neatly down from the fence and landed at Tom's feet.

The kitten looked up at Tom and began to purr. He was her favourite

person on the farm.

Tom picked Nell up, trying not to smile. "You're a naughty girl!" he said. "Poppy could have squashed you!"

"It's not funny," said Hattie.

"No, it's not," agreed Jo. "You know

Poppy's expecting piglets and she mustn't get upset. This is the third time this week that Nell's been inside her pen. Mum will be really cross when she finds out."

Tom sighed. He knew Jo was right, but he found it hard to be angry with Nell. She was such *fun*! Much more interesting than his goldfish, Eric. Tom knew that Hattie and Jo loved Nell too, but not as much as he did.

"Well, we don't have to *tell* Mum," said Tom as he walked back to the house holding Nell tightly, just in case she decided to do something else naughty.

"I bet she'll know anyway," said

Hattie. "Poppy won't stop squealing."

"Mum always knows if Poppy is upset," said Jo. "And she'll guess it was Nell again."

"But promise you won't tell her," shouted Tom over the noise of his mother's tractor coming into the farmyard.

"We won't," said Hattie and Jo.

Tom took Nell into the kitchen and put her into her basket. "Now you stay there," he said, trying to be stern. "Don't muck around any more today!"

Nell didn't like it when Tom was cross. "Can't we play with my toy mouse?" she miaowed.

But Tom still looked serious.

Nell sat back in her basket and yawned. She decided to give herself a bit of a wash. But before long, she fell asleep.

Tom got up and looked out of the window. He watched his mum get down from the tractor and look into the pigpen. Hattie and Jo were shaking their heads solemnly.

"I hope Poppy's all right," Tom muttered to himself as his mum marched across the farmyard towards the kitchen.

The kitchen door opened and Mrs Morgan stomped into the house.

"Hi Mum," said Tom warily.

"Where's that cat?" replied Mrs Morgan.

"She's not a cat, Mum, she's only a kitten," said Tom. He went over to the cat basket where Nell was fast asleep.

"And she's too young to understand about pigs," said Hattie, coming into the kitchen.

"And she's usually really good, isn't she, Tom?" added Jo.

"Yes, she is," said Tom. "She's just not used to being on a farm yet, that's all, Mum."

Mrs Morgan pulled off her boots and flopped down at the kitchen table. She

217

looked tired. "Put the kettle on, Tom love," she said.

Tom filled the kettle with water and plugged it in.

Mrs Morgan wriggled her toes and put her feet up on a chair.

"Well," she said, "I know Nell is only a kitten but she's come here to be a farm cat."

"I know, Mum," said Tom.

His mum carried on, "That means not jumping in the animal feed. And not pulling straw out of the bales. And not chasing the ducks and pouncing on the animals. Especially the pigs. And *especially* Poppy."

"I know, Mum," Tom said again. "Nell *will* learn to be a good farm cat. I'm *sure* she will," he added, crossing his fingers for luck.

The kettle boiled and Mrs Morgan got up to make herself a cup of tea. She poured out some orange juice for Tom, Hattie and Jo and then sat down again, looking worried. "The thing is, I don't want Nell to upset Poppy again," she said. "Poppy is due to have her piglets next week, and if she's upset, she may not look after them properly."

Tom's heart thumped hard. Was his mum hinting that Nell might have to leave the farm? He had to think fast. "We could keep her inside until Poppy has had her piglets," he suggested. "She could stay in my bedroom. I'd make sure she stayed in – honestly Mum! And I'd feed her and empty her litter tray and look after her and—"

"All right," laughed Mrs Morgan. "You can keep Nell in your room until Poppy has had her piglets, OK?"

"Thanks, Mum!" Tom grinned. It would be great to have Nell sleep in his room. He often crept down to the kitchen at night to see if she was all right.

Tom picked up the cat basket and carefully carried it upstairs.

Nell stirred and gave a little miaow. In her dreams she was flying through the air.

Tom had just reached his bedroom door when Hattie bounded up behind him.

"It's not fair you having Nell," Hattie

221

said, grabbing the basket.

"We want to have her too," said Jo, coming up behind Hattie.

"Well, Mum said she could go in *my* room," said Tom, trying to grab the basket back.

"No, in ours," his sisters hissed.

"Mine!"

"*Ours!*" Hattie tugged the basket and Nell tumbled onto the floor. She woke up with a start and shot off into Tom's room and hid under his bed.

"See. She likes my room the best anyway," said Tom.

"No she doesn't!" said Hattie crossly, still holding the basket.

"You just scared her, that's all," said Jo.

"Didn't."

"Did."

"*Stop it*, you three!" Mrs Morgan yelled up the stairs. "Tom, are you looking after that kitten?"

"Yes, Mum!" yelled Tom.

"Good!" shouted Mrs Morgan.

Hattie pushed the basket back at Tom and stuck her tongue out.

Tom crossed his eyes and if he hadn't been holding the basket he would have stuck his fingers up his nose too. He waited until Hattie and Jo had clumped off downstairs and then he went into his room and closed the door.

He scooped Nell out from under his bed, brushed some fluff off her nose and cuddled her tightly. "You've got to be good from now on, Nell," he said.

"Miaow," replied Nell.

"I mean it," said Tom, trying to be stern again but not doing very well.

Nell saw Tom was smiling and licked his hand. She liked being in Tom's room. She snuggled down and went back to sleep.

Chapter Two

When Tom woke up the next morning he found Nell curled up on the pillow beside him. Suddenly there was a hammering on the door and Hattie and Jo burst into the room.

Tom sat up with a start and Nell hid under the duvet.

"There are *ten* of them!" shouted

Hattie, dancing round the room.

"And they're so sweet!" yelled Jo as she leapt onto Tom's bed.

And they're so loud! thought Nell. She poked her nose out from under the duvet and sniffed. There was a smell around Jo and Hattie that reminded her of something. It reminded her of . . . PIG. Nell sneezed.

"Phew," said Tom to Hattie and Jo, "You both smell of . . ."

"*Piglets!*" said Jo.

"Piglets?" asked Tom. 'You mean Poppy's had her . . ."

"Piglets!" Hattie and Jo squealed like a couple of big piglets themselves.

227

They rushed out of the bedroom and slammed the door behind them.

Tom sighed and snuggled back down in bed. Sometimes his sisters were so noisy he wished he had earplugs, or a soundproof bedroom, or even better, a sisterproof bedroom.

When he was sure that Hattie and Jo had gone away, Tom got out of bed. He wanted to see if the piglets were all right. He was a bit worried that the piglets had arrived so early and hoped that it wasn't Nell's fault.

Tom got dressed, gave Eric some fish food and left Nell fast asleep on his pillow. He was soon outside in the morning sunshine.

"Morning, Tom." Mrs Morgan popped her head up over the wall of the pigpen.

"Morning, Mum!" said Tom. "Is Poppy OK?" he asked anxiously. "I mean, the piglets . . . well, they were early and I wondered if it was because of Nell . . ."

Tom's mum opened the gate to the pigpen for Tom to come in and look. She was smiling broadly. "They're all just fine, Tom. I don't think Nell did any harm. Poppy probably had them early because it is such a big litter. She's never had so many piglets before and she's looking after them very well. Isn't she clever?"

Mrs Morgan bent down and stroked Poppy's head. Poppy snuffled and snorted while she lay on the straw feeding a long line of tiny, wriggling, pink piglets.

"Wow!" said Tom. "I've never *seen* so many piglets!"

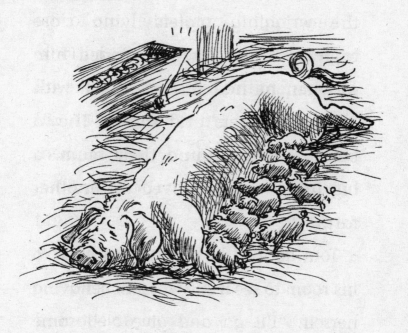

"I'm really pleased," said Mrs Morgan proudly. "And how is Nell? Was she good last night?"

"Really good," said Tom. "I think

she's going to behave from now on,"
he added hopefully. He looked at
the wriggling piglets lying close
to their mum. They reminded him
of when he had first seen Nell with
all her brothers and sisters. They'd
been gathered round their mum, a
big tabby cat that lived on another
farm.

Tom decided he'd better get back to
his room to see if she was still behaving
herself. "I'll go and give Nell some
breakfast, Mum," he said.

"OK, Tom," Mrs Morgan said. "But
I think we need to keep Nell indoors
today, until Poppy has got used to

her new litter. Nell can come back out tomorrow."

"Great," said Tom, smiling happily. All he had to do was make sure Nell stayed out of trouble from now on.

Easy! Tom thought as he walked back to the kitchen to get Nell's breakfast.

Impossible! he thought a few minutes later, when he opened his bedroom door. There was Nell, perched on the edge of a shelf just above the fish tank, staring at Eric.

Oh, no! Tom realised he must have left the lid off Eric's tank again.

Inside the fish tank was one very scared goldfish.

Nell was just dipping a paw into the water when she glanced up and saw Tom. "Hello," she miaowed. "Just doing a spot of fishing!"

"Nell!" yelled Tom. As soon as he said it he knew he shouldn't have.

Suddenly Nell forgot where her front paws were and they slipped and slid – then fell – straight into the fish tank. The rest of Nell followed. *Splash!*

Chapter Three

"Youuwwll!" Nell cried. The wet stuff was *horrible*.

Inside his underwater castle, Eric the goldfish had decided to play dead. For a goldfish, Eric was quite bright.

Tom ran over to the tank and scooped Nell out. Holding the dripping kitten under one arm, Tom used his other hand to touch Eric gently.

Eric flicked his tail and shot out from his castle.

Tom breathed a sigh of relief, but was cross with himself. His mum was always telling him not to leave the lid off Eric's tank. He put the lid back on firmly, then went to the airing cupboard for an old towel to rub Nell dry.

"Thanks for rescuing me, Tom," Nell mewed weakly. She looked up at him, but Tom didn't smile. Nell felt miserable.

Tom wrapped Nell in a rather rough, threadbare towel then carried her down to the kitchen where it was warmer.

"Cats are meant to be afraid of water, not jump into it!" he said sternly as he rubbed her dry. Nell looked very small and skinny with her wet fur.

Tom did smile then. "You look like a little rat," he said, "except I've never seen a tabby rat before."

Nell began to feel better. Her fur felt warmer and less heavy. She yawned. All the excitement had made her tired, so she curled up in her towel and went to sleep.

Tom put Nell down by the radiator and was about to go and top up Eric's tank with water when Hattie and Jo came in, carrying two almost full trays of eggs from the hens.

"Look at all the eggs we got this morning. Forty-four!" said Hattie.

"Mum was really happy," said Jo.

They stacked them carefully on the table. "We're going out to see Poppy and her piglets now," they told Tom.

"OK," said Tom. He left Nell fast asleep by the radiator and shot off upstairs to sort out Eric.

Eric was fine. He was happily swimming around in about 10 centimetres of water, wondering what had happened to the rest of it. Eric had already forgotten about Nell falling in. Although Eric had a good memory for a goldfish, he still forgot *everything* after about five minutes.

Tom filled up the fish tank, gave Eric some more fish food and made sure he put the lid on. Then he heard the crash.

Tom bounded down the stairs,

expecting the worst. And he was right. Nell was on the kitchen table. On the kitchen floor were one upturned tray and a couple of dozen smashed eggs.

"Oh, Nell, look what you've done!" gasped Tom, staring in horror at the oozing, slimy mess.

Nell looked at Tom's face and thought she'd better get off the table. As she sprang down, Hattie burst into the kitchen.

"Mum wants her coat – aagh!" Hattie skidded on the eggs and banged right into the draining board. A glass and two cereal bowls toppled to the floor with a clatter as Hattie came to a halt.

"Oh no," groaned Tom.

"What a mess!" shouted Mrs Morgan when she ran in to see what was happening. "What has been going on?"

"Wow!" breathed Jo as she rushed in too, not wanting to be left out.

Nell sat crouched in the corner on her threadbare towel and looked at Tom's mum.

Tom's mum looked at Nell. "Did Nell do this?" she demanded.

"Not all of it," miaowed Nell, beginning to lick her paws, which were sticky with egg. All this noise and fuss – she wished more than anything that she was still safely asleep in her basket up in Tom's room.

"Well, Tom? Did she?" asked Mrs Morgan sternly.

"Sort of . . . I suppose . . ." Tom said reluctantly.

"I thought so," said his mum. "That kitten is nothing but trouble! I don't think she'll ever make a good farm cat. We won't have a farm left if she carries on like this!" Mrs Morgan sighed. "I really think Nell may have to go and live somewhere else," she said quietly.

"No, Mum!" cried Tom.

Nell looked down at her eggy paws, feeling very miserable.

243

"But Mum, Nell didn't break the crockery," said Hattie. "I knocked it all on the floor when I slipped on the eggs."

"And I'm sure Nell didn't *mean* to break the eggs, Mum," said Tom. "Please give her another chance. *Please!*"

"Please!" said Hattie and Jo.

Mrs Morgan looked at the three pleading faces. "All right," she said, sighing again. "One more chance. Just one! But that's it, OK?"

"OK, Mum," said Tom, smiling in relief.

While Hattie and Jo helped Tom clear up the broken eggs and smashed crockery, Mrs Morgan went out to feed the pigs.

Nell sat quietly under the radiator and carried on cleaning her paws.

The kitchen was soon clean and tidy again. Hattie and Jo ran off outside to play.

Tom decided he ought to try and get back in his mum's good books. He'd go and help her with the pigs. "Back soon, Nell," he said. "Be good."

Nell stopped licking her paws and watched the door close behind Tom. Then she watched it swing open again as it came off the latch.

Nell sat and looked at the slight

opening in the kitchen door. Her nose twitched. It was such a lovely warm day and the farmyard sent such interesting smells wafting her way.

She sat there a bit longer. Then she decided. She could be just as good sitting by the open door, couldn't she? She crept over to the doorway and poked her little pink nose out into the sunshine . . .

Chapter Four

Over in Poppy's pen, Tom and his mum were giving Poppy and her piglets some clean straw to lie on. Suddenly a burst of squawking came from the duck pond.

Tom's heart thumped quickly. Nell! He rushed out just in time to see Nell scooting round the pond, chasing all the ducks into the water. He caught the naughty kitten almost at once, but by then Tom's mum had seen what had happened.

"I'll take Nell inside and shut her in my room," said Tom quickly.

Mrs Morgan nodded crossly. "And make sure she stays there this time," she snapped. "I've had quite enough of that kitten today."

Nell could tell that she was in trouble again. Tom took her up to his room and played with her for a while, but Nell could see that he was thinking about something else. After a while, she went over to snooze in the warm sunshine by the window.

Nell *was* right, Tom *was* thinking about something. He was thinking about Nell's last chance and hoping that his mum did not mean what she had said.

But that evening, when Tom was on his way to clean his teeth, he heard his mum and dad talking in the kitchen.

"Tom will be very upset," Tom's dad was saying. "He's become especially fond of Nell."

"I know," sighed Tom's mum, "but that kitten is never going to settle down here. It would be kinder to let Julie take Nell now so that she can get used to a new home while she's still young."

"Maybe . . ." said Mr Morgan. "But let's give it just a little bit longer, just for Tom."

"You're a big softie," Tom heard his mum say. "OK, one last chance, then."

Tom rushed back to Nell. He picked her up and hugged her tightly. "From now on you really, *really* have to stop being so naughty, Nell," he told her. "Otherwise you have to go and live with Auntie Julie."

Nell was having a strange dream about being hugged by a talking pig. She gave a muffled miaow.

Tom smiled. He loved Auntie Julie, but there was no way she was going to have Nell . . .

The next day was hot and sunny. Tom's mum and dad were busy up in the fields turning the hay so that it dried in the sunshine.

Nell was sitting quietly on Tom's windowsill, gazing out at the sunny farmyard. She stuck her pink nose right up against the window and wished she was outside too, having fun.

Her eyes followed Tom as he walked up to the field where Mr and Mrs Morgan were working. Nell could see Hattie and Jo in the far corner of the field, where they were allowed to play with the hay. They had built a big pile and were jumping into it. It looked like fun!

And now Tom was joining in. Nell yawned and stretched. She wanted some fun too!

She jumped down from the windowsill and went downstairs to explore. But the kitchen door was firmly shut. And so was the door to the sitting-room.

Nell scampered back upstairs. She

looked in the bathroom. Nothing much to play with in there. The next room she came to looked far more interesting . . .

When lunchtime arrived, Mrs Morgan called Tom, Hattie and Jo over. "Hay monsters!" she laughed, as they arrived, picking bits of hay out of their hair and clothes.

"Can I let Nell out for a while, Mum?" Tom asked, as they all walked back to the house together. "I'll stand and watch her, to make sure she doesn't get into any trouble."

Mrs Morgan nodded. "As long as you

do watch her," she said.

Tom smiled back then glanced up at his bedroom window to see if Nell was still looking out. There was no sign of her. Then something caught his eye in the next window along, his mum and dad's bedroom. Tom couldn't quite believe what he saw. Outside it was beautiful sunshine, but inside his mum and dad's room it was snowing.

Chapter Five

"What on earth . . . ?" gasped Mrs Morgan. She had seen it too and began to rush towards the house.

Tom hurried behind her with his dad and sisters. He had an awful feeling that this was something to do with Nell . . .

Mrs Morgan marched through the

kitchen and up the stairs with Tom hot on her heels. She threw open the bedroom door.

Tom squeezed past her into the room. He was right. There in the middle of the big bed, surrounded by a cloud of white feathers, was Nell. She was busily shaking a pillow as though it was a huge white mouse. The other pillow looked crumpled and empty – its feathers already floating around the room.

Nell looked up, saw Tom and was about to purr – but sneezed instead. Then she saw Tom's mum. Mrs Morgan's face was very red and fierce-looking.

Nell knew that she was in big trouble.
She jumped off the bed, shot out of the
room and hid in her basket in Tom's
bedroom.

"They're my best pillows. I don't
believe it. I just don't!" shouted Mrs
Morgan.

"Mum, please, she was bored," Tom
pleaded. "I should have left her a toy to
play with."

"No, Tom," Mrs Morgan replied.
"She's just too naughty and this is the
last straw!"

Nell sat in her basket and listened
miserably to the fuss going on next
door. Soon she heard the sound of Mrs

Morgan's footsteps going downstairs.
Then Tom came in and picked her up.

"Oh, Nell!" he said sadly. "You've really done it this time. Mum's on the phone to Auntie Julie."

Mrs Morgan's voice came floating up the stairs. "I'm so cross! I'm going to have to buy new pillows, Julie . . ." she was saying. "Yes, terrible . . . Tomorrow morning will be fine . . . Thanks, Julie . . . Bye . . . Bye . . ."

Tom sighed and Nell noticed his eyes looked all wet.

Tom didn't want to talk to Auntie Julie when she arrived the next morning.

"Hello, Tom," she said. "I'm really sorry about Nell. You know that you can come and see her any time, don't you? Any time at all."

Tom stared at his feet. It wasn't that

261

he didn't like Auntie Julie. The trouble was that he liked her very much and if she was any nicer to him he had an awful feeling that he might cry. So he kept staring at his feet and said nothing.

"Hattie, Jo," said Mrs Morgan, "why don't you show Auntie Julie the new piglets while Tom says goodbye to Nell?"

"What a good idea," said Auntie Julie, sounding pleased to get out of the kitchen. She ushered Hattie and Jo out of the door.

"Right," said Tom's mum when they had gone. "Let's find Nell and you can say goodbye to her properly."

262

Tom didn't say anything.

"Come on, love," said Mrs Morgan. "Surely you can see that Nell can't stay? And she's only going down the road. You can see her every day at Auntie Julie's if you want to."

"But it won't be the same," Tom mumbled at his shoes.

Mrs Morgan sighed, but she wasn't going to change her mind this time. "Now, where is she?" she asked.

With a heavy heart, Tom went up to his room to fetch Nell. He had left her asleep on his bed when he came downstairs that morning.

But Nell wasn't there. She had gone.

Ten minutes later they still hadn't found Nell.

Tom's mum was getting annoyed. "Are you hiding that kitten somewhere?" she asked Tom.

"No," Tom replied truthfully. It was a good idea and he wished he'd thought of it, but he had no idea where Nell was either.

Crossly, Mrs Morgan called Hattie and Jo in to help search for Nell. Soon they were turning the house upside down.

"She's been here," called out Hattie, "cos my drawing paper's got footprints on it."

"And here," said Jo. "Look, she's eaten my chocolate."

"You ate that yourself, silly," said Hattie, scornfully.

Tom was beginning to wonder if Nell really had disappeared.

Chapter Six

Out by the pigpen, huddled inside an upturned tin bucket, Nell kept as quiet as a mouse. When Mrs Morgan had taken her basket out of Tom's room that morning, Nell had guessed that something not very nice was going to happen to her.

Nell had crept downstairs, and when

Tom's Auntie Julie had arrived, she had scooted outside unnoticed. She watched and waited, listening unhappily to the sounds going on around her.

"We can't find her anywhere," sighed Hattie and Jo.

Tom watched Auntie Julie through the window as she fussed around the pigpen. He was beginning to hope that Nell would disappear long enough for Auntie Julie to give up waiting and go home. He threw himself down on the sofa and sighed.

A moment later Auntie Julie came back in. Mrs Morgan shook her head to let her know that they hadn't found Nell.

Auntie Julie shrugged her shoulders, then sat down at the kitchen table.

"You can't hide Nell forever," Mrs Morgan told Tom crossly.

"I'm *not* hiding her!" Tom cried.

Out by the pigpen, Nell's nose twitched. Something was wrong. She peeped around the edge of the bucket and saw a little pink bottom with a curly tail rush by. It was one of the piglets. What was it doing out of the pigpen?

Nell crept out of the bucket to see more piglets running from the pen,

while their mother snuffled about in the chicken feed. The pigpen gate hadn't been closed properly. As she watched, one of the piglets squeezed under the front gate and ran down the lane.

Nell was worried. She liked to tease the other farm animals, but she didn't want to see any of them hurt. And that piglet was going to get into big trouble, running off like that!

Nell dashed over to the house – but the kitchen door was closed! She jumped onto the stone ledge under the kitchen window. Tom and his sisters, and his mum and Auntie Julie were all sitting round the table, talking.

"Tom! Tom – come out! Come and look!" Nell miaowed loudly, scratching on the windowpane as she called.

Everyone looked up.

"Catch her!" shouted Mrs Morgan, pushing her chair back and dashing outside, closely followed by Tom.

Then Mrs Morgan saw that the piglets were out of their pen. "Oh no!" she cried, forgetting about Nell. "Catch them!" she yelled.

Everyone began to run around the yard, herding the piglets safely back into the pen. But Nell ran over to the front gate, hoping Tom would follow her.

"Come here, Nell," Tom called, walking towards her.

But Nell ran under the gate and on down the lane.

"Nell! Come back!" Tom called. He quickly climbed over the gate and ran after her.

Just then, Nell spotted the runaway piglet snuffling about in a muddy ditch. She stood there, waiting for Tom to catch up.

At first, Tom couldn't believe his eyes. Nell wasn't being naughty at all. She'd run off to show him one of the farm animals was in trouble!

When Tom's mum spotted him walking back up the lane she called out to him, looking worried. "There's a piglet missing, Tom."

"No there isn't," Tom called back, smiling. He held the piglet up for his mum to see.

Nell walked beside Tom, feeling

pleased. Perhaps she was a real farm cat now.

But Mrs Morgan didn't see it that way. She briskly picked Nell up and tucked her under her arm. "I might have known you'd be right in the middle of trouble," she said to Nell crossly.

"Mum . . ." protested Tom.

"Oh, that's not fair," Auntie Julie told her sister. "All this was my fault, not Nell's."

"Your fault?" asked Mrs Morgan, puzzled.

Auntie Julie went a little pink. "I must have left the pigpen gate open. Sorry."

"And Mum," said Tom, "if Nell hadn't come and scratched on the window at us, all the piglets might have got out on the road!"

"Oh don't, Tom," said Mrs Morgan, looking pale.

"So Nell wasn't being naughty at all this time," Jo said brightly.

Tom smiled at his sister. "That's right. Nell knew what was happening, Mum," he said. "She came and got us – and then she led me straight to the piglet that had run off down the lane!"

"Now Nell's a proper farm cat," said Harriet, happily.

"So I think we should keep her, Mum," Tom said quietly.

Harriet and Jo nodded hard.

Mrs Morgan looked at Auntie Julie to see what she thought.

"Tom's right," said Auntie Julie. "I

think Nell will be a good farm cat, after all."

"Yes, I will," miaowed Nell, wriggling in Mrs Morgan's arms. "Now can you stop squashing me, please?"

Mrs Morgan untucked the wriggling kitten from under her arm and gave her to Tom, smiling. "Then I suppose she can stay."

"*Really?*" asked Tom.

"Really," laughed Mrs Morgan.

Hattie and Jo cheered and Tom hugged Nell tight, a huge smile on his face.

As Nell purred happily in Tom's arms, two ducks waddled past. Nell's tail twitched. She was tempted, but she wasn't going to chase them. No – she was going to enjoy being a good farm cat – for today, at least . . .

Out now!

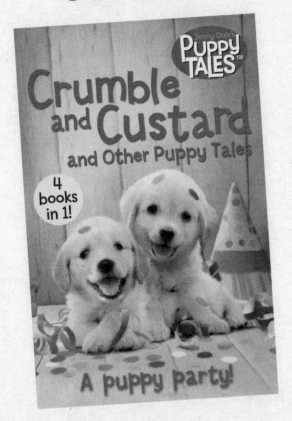

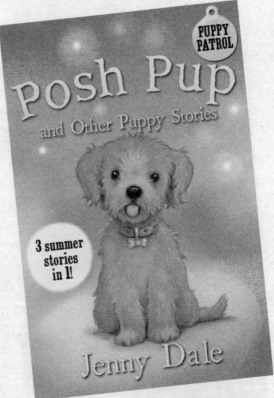